Skirt Chaser

FILTHY DIRTY LOVE #2

STACEY KENNEDY

Stacey Kennedy
www.staceykennedy.com

Edited by Christa Soule
Copy Edited by Chelle Olson, Literally Addicted to Detail
Cover Photograph & Cover Design by Sara Eirew
Print Edition Graphic Fantastic

Manufactured in Canada
First Edition August 2017

As always, for my readers.

Chapter 1

She's a goddamn temptress.

Downtown Seattle, in a high-rise that offered views of Elliott Bay, the Space Needle, and the Seattle Great Wheel, Greyson Crawford held back a groan. Sitting behind his grand desk in his corner office, he watched as Evie Richards bent down, picking up the piece of paper that had fallen to the ground. The heat to his groin was swift and unbearable, and he bit the inside of his cheek, fighting against the brutal hardening of his cock. He couldn't quite put a finger on what was so spectacular. Maybe her long, flowing, blond hair? Her curvaceous, hourglass figure? Her piercing, light green eyes? Whatever it was, she was pure temptation dressed in a proper, professional, black dress that he wanted to rip the fuck off her.

One month.

Thirty days.

Seven hundred and twenty hours.

No matter how he looked at it, the past days working alongside her had been a horrendous torture. He'd slowly been counting down this day to come. The day that Evie's contract with his company, Crawford Architecture, was done. Soon, she'd move on, ready to wow some other big company in Seattle that needed her on-point interior design expertise.

Today was the day that he could officially seduce her into his bed.

As she rose, righting her skirt to its proper, knee-length place, he wanted nothing more than to yank that skirt over her hips and redden that round ass a little. Through the glass wall separating his office from the main area with its large cubicles for his engineering and design staff, he watched her move to the temporary desk she'd been given, and reach for her cell phone by her keyboard.

For one month now, he'd endeavored to keep their relationship professional. Grey knew the rules. One, don't mix business and pleasure. Two, keep his hands off his employees. Throughout her contract, he'd teased her with a little light flirtation to let his interest be known. He'd never crossed the line, though. Soon, he would. But until she left his office today, officially ending her contract, he had to wait. Patiently. Like a lion ready to take its prey.

Right then, she placed her phone back on the desk, tears filling her eyes. Even from where he sat, he could see the tremble in her hands. There was a stillness about her that raised his mental alarms, as her eyes were frozen on the screen.

Grey began to rise from his seat, as Janet, his longtime assistant, suddenly approached Evie's desk. His eyes were only on Evie, and when she spotted Janet, tears flooded her face, her mouth moving with words that Grey couldn't hear.

Janet reached out, placing a comforting hand on Evie's shoulder.

His back straightened like a steel rod, and he was striding to his door and out of the office before his next breath. He didn't get there in time, and before he could reach her cubicle, Evie suddenly ran into the hallway and past him, her makeup trailing black lines down her face.

Determined to get answers, he moved toward her desk, finding Janet staring down at Evie's cell phone. "What was that all about?" he asked.

"Oh," Janet said in her high-pitched voice, her short, blond bob hiding her round face as she picked up Evie's phone. "I guess her best friend is engaged to her ex-boyfriend, and this weekend they're having a destination wedding." She spun the phone around, showing Grey the screen, displaying a photo of a blond woman wearing nothing but a bright red string bikini. Next to her, a brown-haired guy rested an arm possessively around the woman's shoulders. *Can't wait for you to get here!* was written in bold red letters at the bottom of the photo. "Evie is the maid of honor."

Janet handed him the phone, and as he gazed upon the woman, he said, "Let me get this straight. Evie is the maid of honor in her best friend's wedding who is marrying Evie's ex-boyfriend?"

Janet gave a tight smile and nodded. "Now you understand why she's upset. I think the reality of it all maybe just hit her."

"I suppose that explains the tears," Grey surmised.

Janet nodded, a scowl marring her usually sweet face. "Poor girl, if these are the people she has in her life."

Grey stared down at the photo before the screen went black, confused. Evie didn't seem the type to allow anyone to make her feel small. Christ, her confidence was one of the things he found so damn titillating. "Leave this with me," he told Janet, holding up the phone. "I'll see that she gets it back."

"Oh, I'm sure you will," Janet said, pointing a long, red-painted fingernail at him. "Don't you dare make her more upset. She is a very sweet girl. She's not like your usuals."

"I'm well aware," Grey retorted, shoving his hand into his pocket, not at all insulted. Janet, as well as Grey's closest friend, Maddox Hunt, a cop with the Seattle Police Department, might be the only two people who knew him enough to know that statement was warranted.

Sometime back in college, with a reputation that followed him into his thirty-fifth year now, he'd been called a skirt-chasing ladies' man. He had lived up to that name, and he didn't make apologies for it either. He liked women, usually only once, but sometimes more than one at a time. Sure, he'd done the relationship thing before, but women tended to get a) clingy and b) boring.

Not Evie.

She tempted him in ways no one had. And it wasn't just the game of playing hard to get. There was something different about this woman…something that made him count down the days until she stopped working for him.

"All right, as long as we've got that clear," Janet said, giving a tender smile, patting Grey's arm. "Be gentle with this one."

When Janet headed back to her desk outside of Grey's office, he looked back to the black screen on the phone. What kind of thoughtless friend would not only date an ex but then ask you to stand up for the wedding? There had to be more to the story.

Determined to get to the bottom of it, and erase those tears the bastards had caused, he kept Evie's phone in his hand and then moved down the hallway, looking for her. Midway down the corridor, he noticed that his CFO's assistant, Trina, was glancing at the women's washroom. "Did Evie go in there?" he asked Trina when he reached her.

"Yeah," Trina said with a soft nod. "She seemed upset."

Grey glanced at the closed black door with the woman's washroom logo. "Is anyone else in there?"

"I can't be sure since I haven't really been paying attention, but I don't think so."

Good enough for him. "I'd appreciate it if you could ensure that no one else goes in until I come out."

Trina didn't even bat an eye. "Yes, sir."

Of course, she wouldn't. Grey was her boss, and this was certainly none of her business. Even if his company had typical office gossip, and he knew word of this would get around, no one would ever dare chatter to his face.

Intent and careful to take his time not to scare any other employees in the restroom, he entered the simple and modern bathroom with the five stalls. Only one door was closed, and there was no one at the sink, so he moved toward the vanity and leaned against it. Hands shoved into his pockets, he stared at the closed door, giving Evie the time she needed. That's when he heard her soft cries, and with those pained noises, something inside of him tensed.

It was a sensation strong enough to make him question what it was about this woman that drew him in so intently. She'd gotten a grip on his mind and body so tightly that he pondered her situation, and his, and what he could do about both. He'd become so lost in his thoughts that he didn't realize she'd opened the door until she was leaving the stall and striding out.

Head down, she hadn't noticed him yet, so he called out to her, "Evie."

A scream ripping from her throat, hands pressing against her chest. "Holy shit!"

He couldn't help but chuckle. "I'm sorry for scaring you." His amusement washed away when he took a good look at her face. There was so much pain there. He didn't like it.

The shock from her face slowly faded. "Why are you in here?" she asked.

"To return your phone to you." He moved to her, watching her following his every step. The heat in her eyes was instant, and that'd always been the problem. She wanted him. Christ, did she want him, he could tell. But she was smart and clever, never one to cross the professional line either. She was also a good girl, who likely needed love before sex. Maybe that was the real reason she didn't ever cross the line. Maybe it was less about the job and more about protecting her heart from a guy that screamed *danger*. He could understand why

Though he never was a man who took the easy road, and he sure as shit liked a challenge. He stared into her gorgeous eyes, and a plan formed. One that got him what he wanted, and yet would benefit her, too. He'd never been a sly or shady guy, but he was a good businessman. And that meant using a situation to his advantage.

"So, that's it. You got out the good cry you needed to," he said to her, and he liked the way her lips parted when he leaned in toward her; it showed him just how much she yearned for his kiss. "Your ex is marrying your best friend," he added. "He's an asshole. She's a bitch. This is happening, but it's how you deal with it that truly matters."

"He's not an asshole," she said softly, shaking her head. "And she's not a bitch. I've helped plan their wedding for the last year, and I'm happy for them. I think...maybe it hadn't sunk in or something." She drew in a deep breath, releasing it out her nose and added with a soft smile, "But I'm better now. I'm sorry I fell apart out there."

"One, I disagree with you," he retorted sternly. "I'm not convinced these aren't terrible people. And two, do not apologize that their selfishness hurt you. In fact, I'd say it's time to get revenge, don't you think?"

The side of her mouth arched slightly. He noted her long exhale, and he knew that had nothing to do with emotions. That it was this push and pull thing going on between them. Call it chemistry, intensity, whatever, it was as addictive as it was captivating. "How exactly do I do that?" She grabbed a paper towel, got it a bit wet with cold water, and then began wiping off her makeup, adding, "Murder them?" She gave him her sexy smile that pooled heat in his groin.

Grey chuckled, leaning his hip against the counter. "Perhaps that's a bit extreme. Murder means jail time, and you going away is definitely not what I want."

She slowly glanced at him then, cheeks flushing pink, and the dilation of her pupils was obvious. That look had snagged him the very first day after his COO hired her to design the lobby of the interior of their latest multi-million-dollar high-rise.

Now, the look intensified, hardening his cock, centering his mind on all the wicked things he'd like to do to her. He stepped toward her, as she spun around, leaning against the counter, wide eyes on him. There was something about her, maybe her innocence, maybe this unexplainable connection that had only grown since he worked alongside her, but it captured him in an unbreakable spell.

In the seconds that passed, the desire practically wafted off her, scented so sweet his cock went hard just that easily. As it always did, the space between them felt charged with electricity, but he'd never gotten this close to her before. He never let her feel the extent of how he wanted her. Now, he held nothing back.

"I have a better idea than jail time," he told her, giving her enough distance that if she wanted to move and leave the bathroom, she could. When she stayed put, he added, "Show these bastards up. Take me with you, and make them both ragingly jealous."

Her eyes searched his, then she broke out in loud laughter. "Yeah, right. Hilarious."

She might have said one thing, but the only thing he noticed was that she wasn't moving, eyes locked on him. "I'm not kidding," he said, erasing the distance between them, placing both hands on either side of her, trapping her between him and the counter.

"You're not kidding," she said, more of a statement than a question.

Grey glanced from her bottom lip she nibbled to her flushed cheeks to her smoldering eyes... Christ, what he'd do to this woman. It would be indecent. "I would never joke about something that so clearly upsets you," he told her seriously. "I can only imagine you want to one-up them. I know I would. Use me to do it."

"She's my best friend," she said softly. "I don't need to one-up her."

He let his gaze roam over her pretty face before looking into her smoldering eyes again. "Tell me it's never crossed your mind what it would feel like to walk in there not like a sad third wheel but like a woman who owns the world."

"And how would that ever happen?'

"You'll have me on your arm."

Her mouth twisted. "You're pretty sure of yourself."

"Angel, I am never the third wheel of anything," he told her, dead serious. "I'm the engine, the accelerator, and the whole damn car."

She swallowed deeply and studied him, *hard*. "All right," she eventually said, "say I'm game and actually agree to this crazy plan, what do you get out of it?"

"I get you." He brought his mouth close enough to tease her. She wanted his kiss, angling her head backward, parting her lips. He dragged his nose across hers, and added, "I get to have you in all the ways you know I want you. Beneath me, over me, against a wall, on your knees, screaming my name, whatever I want. Completely under my control." And to ensure there were no misunderstandings, he sternly added, "My game. My rules. Your surrender, until we're back in Seattle."

In a breathy voice, she asked, "Tell me why any sane woman would do this?"

He grinned at her—a sly smile that worked its charm on many women but seemed to have an even greater effect on her. He watched the way the heat rippled through her, and her breath grew rough and raspy, and fuck, did he want to make her moan.

"First, and most importantly," he answered, staying on point, "*you* will do this because we both know you've been looking for a good reason to say yes to a little guilt-free, no-strings-attached with me. So, here it is. I'm giving you the perfect scenario for us to make that happen. The rules are clear. There can be no misunderstandings."

She hadn't blinked. "And second?"

"Secondly," he said, moving his nose to her neck, inhaling her scent of sugar and spice while he slid back up her smooth skin to her ear, feeling her shuddering under his touch. "I'm that guy that every woman, including your bitch of a best friend, will want." He lifted his head, staring into her lust-filled eyes. "I'm the perfect guy to show your shithead ex-boyfriend you've moved up in the world."

She finally blinked. "When exactly would this arrangement start?"

"Tonight. My house. Eight o'clock. Bring your suitcase." He paused, considered his next steps. "Send your flight and resort details to my email so I can get that squared away."

She nodded. "Okay."

He took her chin, tilting her eyes to lock onto his. "The proper reply is: 'Yes, Grey, I agree to your terms.'"

Silence fell.

A slowly seductive, delicious darkness slid over her eyes with her grin. "Yes, Grey, I agree to your terms."

Chapter 2

Later that night, Evie passed through security of an upscale condominium located in a prime spot in downtown Seattle and then stopped in the marble lobby waiting for the elevator to return. With her suitcase at her side, she held her cell phone in her hand, reading the text from her assistant, and her good friend, Monica.

Don't worry about a thing. The signed Henderson contract came in, and we don't start until next Thursday so stop thinking about work. I'll email if anything comes up. Enjoy your mini-trip with your future husband.

The Henderson contract was even bigger than the one Crawford Architecture had offered her, and life for her little, five-year-old company, consisting of her, Monica, and her receptionist, Angie, had been looking pretty great over the past year. But work was so far from her mind. She now regretted telling Monica about her deal with Grey and texted back: *You are so NOT funny!*

Yes, I am, and you love me for it!

Evie laughed, right as the elevator doors chimed and opened. She stuck her cell back into her purse and entered the elevator, moving to the back, glad she opted for a light dinner. The ground vanished as she whizzed up to the twenty-seventh floor, the windows along the exterior of the elevator showing her just how far up she was going.

When the elevator stopped, and the doors began to open, she released her death grip on the railing and grabbed her suitcase, rolling it behind her as she looked up, finding warm gray eyes regarding her. She took in all six-foot-two inches of Greyson Crawford. Dark-blond-haired, perfectly muscular, with a half sleeve of gray and black tattoos covering his right arm, he was what boys hoped to be when they grew up. But Grey also had something no other guy Evie had met before possessed, passion…and a lot of it.

From day one, she knew she couldn't date a guy like Grey. The kind of man who made women fall in love with him because he was perfectly perfect in every way and then left them in broken pieces later because he couldn't commit. He was *that* guy: rich, sexy as hell, and sensually delectable. But he was the type her mother always warned her about.

Yet she'd agreed to this deal for all the reasons he'd offered. For the past month, she'd craved him in ways that no woman should desire any man. He'd filled her dreams, both at night and during the day. She'd watched the way his mouth moved when he spoke and wondered how those lips would feel against her skin. She often studied his hands when he slid them over blueprints, aching to feel that touch between her thighs. His passion for his work, his detail, his focus, it was the sexiest thing she'd ever seen. Saying yes to Grey had been inevitable. With his arrangement, he'd given her a way to be with him with no strings attached. For a limited amount of time that would allow her to protect her heart. She knew what this was and what it wasn't. They could have a fling in paradise, then she'd return to reality, and life would go on. The perfect fantasy.

Only an idiot would say no to that offer. She was no idiot. And she was damn certain Grey would give her the best sex of her life.

"All packed and ready to go?" Grey asked, snapping her away from her thoughts.

"I am." She nodded. "You?"

"Just about," he replied, leaning against the post separating the foyer and the living room. "I need to print off our boarding passes, and then I'll be ready to go."

"Did you add yourself to my room at the resort?" she asked, pushing the handle of the suitcase down.

The smile he gave screamed *up to no good*. "I did."

She pondered exactly what the expression could mean when he offered his hand, and her mind cleared of thoughts. She stared at his hand, wondering how the game would be played. Would he take her to the bedroom now? Or take her right here against the wall like he said he planned to?

Warmth pooled low in her body, and she noted the tremble in her hand. He obviously saw too by the curve of his mouth as she placed her hand in his. He slowly, in a way that almost seemed calculated, tugged her toward him. God, the seconds passed like damn minutes, and her nipples puckered. Skirt-chasing ladies' man or not, when a guy like Grey looked at you, your body stood up and took notice, and hers was screaming *fuck me now!*

Her heart raced, and she angled her chin back, ready for his kiss, when he leaned down and took her suitcase from her, placing it on

17

the floor. "Come on. Let's get you a drink." He gave her a wink and a knowing smile she'd grown fond of these past weeks.

God, how did he control her body like that? One second, she wasn't even thinking about sex. The next, she wanted him desperately. She exhaled a long breath, watched him head down a couple of stairs which led to an open concept living room, with the kitchen off to the left side. When he glanced over his shoulder with those smoky, smoldering eyes, she wondered if grabbing and humping him was against the rules?

She slipped out of her high heels and followed him into the living room, noting that while Grey lived on the penthouse floor, and this condo was totally out of her price range, the condo did seem a bit on the small side for a man she knew came from a mega-rich family. Sure, it offered 270-degree views of the Olympics, Space Needle, city lights, and Mount Rainier, but there were places far pricier than this one in the city.

The space was simply decorated with modern furnishings, with a small stone bar off to the side near the bank of windows, black leather furniture, a large painting on the wall that she assumed probably cost more than her yearly income, and an unlit fireplace—clearly the focal point of the space.

"Does the design live up to your standards?" Grey asked, stepping behind the bar, reaching for something underneath the black marble countertop.

"Most definitely," she said with a smile. "This room is clean, modern, simplistic. It suits you." She moved to the floor-to-ceiling windows and stared out at the city she loved. "But the view is just…wow."

"It's quite something, isn't it?"

The whimsical tone of his voice surprised her enough to glance back at him. His eyes glistened. She didn't expect Grey to have an appreciation for beautiful things that didn't involve big tits and a tight ass. "Did you build this building?" she asked.

He nodded, returning to his search beneath the bar. "It was my very first building."

"Really?" She looked back out the window to all the sparkling lights below. Sentimental? Another surprise. "Have you lived here since it opened?"

"No." He chuckled, and it was a deep enough sound that it drew her gaze again. "When this building was built, I think I had probably a thousand dollars in my bank account."

He placed a bottle of red wine on top of the bar and pointed to it. She nodded. "Please, and I also find you having no money very hard to believe."

Eyebrow arched, he uncorked the wine. "Why is that?"

"Because you're Greyson Crawford, son of mega-rich Anne Crawford."

He reached beneath the bar again then placed two wine glasses on the countertop before he poured the wine into one. "Which is important to this conversation because…?"

"Because you come from a wealthy family."

His lips pressed into a firm line as he began pouring the second glass. "I've never used my mother's money."

"Ever?"

"Well, I can't say ever." He recorked the wine then returned to her with both glasses in his hands. "She paid for my education, but beyond that, no."

"Oh." She accepted the glass he offered her, pondering that revelation, wondering if she should believe him or not.

He sipped his wine and then laughed. "I might take offense to how surprised you look."

"Well…" She gave a shrug, knowing she had nothing to lose by telling him the truth. That's what she liked about this deal between them. She could be herself without worries she'd offend him. "It is surprising, I guess."

"A good surprise or bad?"

"Good," she admitted.

"Well, then, I'm glad." His mouth twitched when he tilted his wine glass toward her. "Because now that you realize I'm not a bastard who would take his mother's money, and that maybe you don't know everything about me just yet so it's best to stop making judgments, we can move on, yes?"

A laugh bubbled up from her throat. Of all the ways she thought her first non-work-related conversation with Greyson Crawford might go, *this* certainly hadn't been what she expected. Charming and sweet, who was this guy? Where was the brutal, cutthroat, skirt-chasing ladies' man that the women at his office talked about?

Regardless, she needed to stay on her toes. He'd likely gained a lot of notches on his bedpost using all that charm. Sex with Grey was one thing. A relationship was something else entirely. And not something she wanted to entertain.

She sipped her wine, regarding him, savoring the woodsy hints. "Just so we're clear," she said, calling him out, showing him she wasn't easily won over, "are you implying that the way you're perceived is generally wrong?"

"No, I imagine that most things that are said about me are likely the truth," he said, lifting a shoulder. "But there are parts of me that are mine. That the public doesn't get to see." He gestured to his living room. "This condo—the meaning of why I live here, why I am proud that when I became wealthy enough, I bought this place to remind myself of how much that meant to me—is something that's not public knowledge."

"Well, I suppose I can understand that," she said, tilting her wine glass in acknowledgment that he'd proved his point that maybe she didn't know everything there was to know about Greyson Crawford. At the same time, she also couldn't forget the things she *did* know about him. Like, his habit of changing women like he changed his socks.

"So," he said, leaning his shoulder against the glass wall, staring at her with those warm, smoky eyes. "What about your company? Did your parents help pay for that?"

Okay, point for him. She swallowed the wine in her mouth and gave a tight smile, now realizing how dreadfully awful her question was. "My family doesn't have a lot of money. They're not poor or anything, but very comfortable living in the middle class."

"You've risen to the top then with all your hard work?"

She nodded. "Partly, but I was super lucky to intern with Hilary Goderich."

"Ah," Grey said, a knowing look on his face. "I know Hilary"—he gestured to his living room again—"she's who did this."

"Guess that makes sense," Evie said, laughing. "It's probably why I like this space so much. We have very similar tastes, Hilary and I, and it's why we got along so well."

Grey took another sip of his wine then asked, "How long did you work together?"

"Almost three years," she explained, recalling some very happy times. "One year interning during school, and then she took me under her wing for two more years before she retired. Luckily for me, a lot of her clients came to me in her absence. Call it good timing, or fate, or who knows, but it made my step forward easier."

"Karma," he said, seemingly so sure of that. "Good things happen to good people, that's all that was."

"Possibly," she agreed. Or at least she hoped. For a long time, life hadn't seemed that way. She'd trudged through the murky waters, trying to do the right thing, be the good person she wanted to be, but life often had a way of kicking you in the teeth.

Maybe Grey was her reward for the bad times she'd been through and survived. Perhaps this was karma, and he was here at the right time to help her get through a hard weekend. That thought reminded her that she wanted to get this show on the road. They'd made an agreement. Hell, she wanted *this*…wanted him. She drew in a deep breath and then downed the remainder of her wine before placing her glass on the end table closest to her.

When she turned to him again, she found Grey grinning at her. "So…" she said, pushing past the nerves tickling in her belly. "How do you want to go about this?"

One brow slowly arched. "Go about what exactly?"

Now decided about the weekend, about him, about it all, she had no qualms about taking control of the situation to see it through. "Sex. Are we doing that here or in your bedroom?"

His mouth twitched. "Get right to it, is that what you want?" His eyes danced, softening his usual tough exterior. "All business, then?"

"This is a business arrangement of sorts, is it not?" she countered.

His eyes slowly began to narrow on her, seemingly removing everything else in the room but her. "No, Evie, my wanting to fuck you has nothing to do with a business transaction. This is personal in every way I can possibly think."

Heat flooded her from head to toe, concentrating between her thighs. He turned and placed his wine glass down on the bar, then focused entirely on her, hands in his pockets. Suddenly, the passionate way he watched her made her notice things about him. Like how strong he looked, powerful even. How it seemed like every second that passed, he learned something new about her. And how the probing nature of his stare made her uncomfortable in the best sort of way, somehow making her feel both noticed and desired in one big sweep.

He stepped closer, bringing all his warmth close to hers. "But tell me your position here, Evie. Do you want to fuck me, right now, right here?"

Her lips parted, a soft breath escaping. "Isn't that why I'm here?"

He brought the strength of his body against hers, and he was all she knew as he stared down at her. "It is the arrangement we made, yes." He reached up, pulled the strap of her blouse a little off her shoulder and kissed the skin there. "Shall I bend you over right here and lift your skirt, taking you as I want?"

She shivered against the goose bumps rising on her flesh, her eyes fluttering shut. "That is what you wanted."

He pulled the strap of her blouse down a little farther over her shoulder and placed another open-mouthed kiss there. "Or should I press you against this window, nestle between your thighs, and feast on your pussy until I've had my fill?"

She moaned. His voice…the words…her tummy clenched as desire flooded her.

He dragged his tongue over her shoulder slowly. "And then I'd give you my cock, only after I tasted you. Is that what you want, Evie?"

She quivered with the promise in his voice. He pressed his erection against her thigh, showing her how incredible his cock would be.

"Look at me."

When his hand slid across her cheek, she reopened her eyes and leaned into his touch. His hand was strong, warm, and everything she apparently desired. Whatever he found in her expression caused the side of his mouth to curve. He leaned forward and gently pressed his mouth against hers.

At first, his kiss was teasing. Sometimes licking. Sometimes nibbling with his teeth. Sometimes sucking on her skin. But then everything changed, and his body stiffened, his hand slid from her face to the back of her skull, where he threaded his fingers into her hair, gripping the strands tightly.

She moaned, melting into the hold. He didn't gently coax her anymore, he owned her mouth. He angled her head, deepening the kiss. His tongue dove inside, swirling against hers, his powerful mouth claiming her.

His kiss was everything she didn't know she was missing.

By the time he backed away, keeping his fingers tangled in her hair, and her head angled back so he could gaze into her eyes, she was breathless. He cupped her chin with his other hand, and she felt trapped in a hold oddly safe, changing her in unexpected ways. She didn't know a touch could mean *this* much, but she was melting right down to her toes for him.

His voice lowered, eyes blazed red-hot. "Are you asking me to fuck you, Evie?"

"Yes," she stated, unashamed.

He grinned, devilishly. "Have you forgotten already?"

"Forgotten what?"

His gaze fell to her lips. He brushed a thumb across her damp mouth in a gesture that spoke of his desire. "My game," he stated. "My rules. Your surrender." He stepped back, breaking her out of his spell. The coldness in the air was a shock to her system, when he added, "You can sleep in the spare bedroom, third door on the right. Set your alarm for five o'clock, we're flying out at seven thirty." Without another word, he left the room.

As Evie watched him disappear down the hallway, she finally got it. Likely, what every woman before her got.

Grey wasn't only passion.

He was lust. And control.

And she wanted more.

Chapter 3

The next morning, the plane accelerated down the runway. Grey glanced at the seat next to him when Evie began humming. He couldn't hold back his chuckle, and he arched an eyebrow at her. "The *Star Wars* theme song?"

"Sorry," she said, eyes crinkling with amusement. "I can't help it. It's so fitting, don't you think?"

"You're cute and amusing, that's what I think." He stretched out his legs, thrilled she was smiling again.

This morning when they arrived at the airport, Evie hadn't been particularly happy to learn that when Grey bought his ticket yesterday, he'd upgraded both his and Evie's ticket to first class. She'd taken it personally, probably thinking he was trying to buy her affection. But she'd been wrong. He simply hadn't flown coach in his life, ever, and he didn't plan on squishing himself into the tight seats today for no other reason than to avoid her annoyance.

She squinted at him, all tense in her seat, and then said, "Nope, I can't hold it in." She hummed the song again and then even did the arm movements of an X-wing Starfighter flying in the sky. "Okay, I'm done," she said, laughing, once the plane leveled off.

He chuckled too, impressed that she wasn't more guarded. So many women in his past took themselves so seriously, but she didn't seem to be one of them. He liked that about her. When she needed to be serious, like on the job, she was, but then there was this side of her he'd never seen. Playful, sexy.

"I'm actually surprised you even know the *Star Wars* song," she said, dragging him out of his thoughts.

"Why wouldn't I?" He frowned, a little offended. "Do you honestly find me that stuffy?"

She regarded him, lips pursed, then she finally half shrugged. "Not stuffy necessarily, but not really a guy I'd imagine sitting on the couch, eating popcorn, and watching *Star Wars*." She studied his face and then laughed softly, shaking her head. "Nope, sorry, I can't picture it at all."

"Why is that picture so unbelievable?" He honestly wondered.

"I don't know," she explained, searching his eyes again. "Too busy working. Too busy at fancy dinners. Too busy sipping scotch and smoking cigars." She glanced out the window, having no idea how much those words impacted him.

She wasn't wrong. That was his life, sort of. He'd grown up surrounded by wealth and extravagance and stuffiness of all kinds. Until he met his friend Maddox through another friend. Maddox showed him how true friends were with each other, not angling for some favor or looking to get in good with his mother, but real. He'd also introduced Grey to the world of wild parties and dark, sensual sex clubs of all kinds, including private parties that catered to BDSM.

"I have seen the *Star Wars* movies," he told her, garnering her attention again. "I also liked them…and the popcorn. Honestly, Evie, I'm not as fancy as you think. My closest friend is a cop. I spend more time with him doing normal guy stuff, like eating chicken wings at a bar every Thursday night than drinking scotch and smoking cigars."

"Interesting," was all she said.

He arched an eyebrow at her. "Again, in a good way or bad?"

"Good." She gave a decidedly firm nod. "You're proving very good at surprising me."

"And that's good, too?"

She laughed and nodded softly. "Very good." She glanced out the window, and he could still see her smiling.

Though *his* smile was nowhere to be found. Now that he thought about it, and as his ears popped with the pressure change, he realized this was the first personal trip he'd taken in years. Sure, he'd gone on business trips a couple of times a week for clients who lived in different places across North America, but a personal trip? Not since his buddy Maddox and he went to San Francisco back in college for a fun week at the four luxurious sex clubs they have there.

Breaking into his thoughts, the flight attendant stopped at their seats and asked, "Something to drink?"

Grey glanced at Evie, and she said, "Coffee, please."

"One milk and a little sugar for her," Grey added. "Black for me."

The flight attendant smiled, accepting the order, then moved to the next couple behind them.

When he looked at Evie again, her eyes were narrowed. "And just how do you know how I take my coffee?"

"Because you worked for me."

"Seriously?" she asked, eyes wide. "You remember what I take in my coffee? Damn, Grey"—she leaned her head back against the head-rest and grinned at him—"you better not be too good, or you're going to start making me look bad."

He didn't want to put her in a poor light, but he definitely wanted to make himself look better. He never regretted the man he was or made a single apology for the life he led, but somehow, the way Evie seemed to see him got right under his skin. "So," he said, getting his mind off things he couldn't control at the moment, "tell me the history of the people I'll be meeting this weekend."

She sighed, keeping her head on the headrest, eyes on him. "I guess you need that information, huh?"

"A little backstory would be good for our relationship to be believable."

She hesitated and blinked. "We're in a relationship?"

He nodded. "As far as all the people at the wedding know, we are. You can hardly look like you own the world if all I am is a short-term piece of man candy on your arm."

"So?"

"So we're in a relationship," he confirmed. "No one needs to know it won't go beyond this weekend."

She hesitated. Then, "Oh, my God!"

He wasn't sure what caused her face to tighten like she'd eaten a lemon, but suddenly, she dropped her head into her hands and mumbled something.

"Are you okay?" he asked.

"I can't believe I'm actually doing this," she said, lifting her head and looking at him again, eyes tight, cheeks flushed pink. "I mean, honestly, this entire thing is crazy!"

29

"Why crazy?" he asked, not seeing it that way at all. "There is nothing wrong with sweetening your life a little for this weekend so that you take what could be a shitty situation and make it better for you. At the end of the day, you're not hurting anyone, but lessening the hurt you feel. In my eyes, there is absolutely nothing wrong with that."

She pondered and then sighed, her shoulders lowering. "I suppose you're right."

"Of course, I am." He winked. "Now, tell me more about these people so I understand all this."

Her lips parted to reply, but the flight attendant placed her coffee down on her tray table and then delivered Grey's. "Thanks," she said with a smile to the woman. She sipped her coffee, then explained to Grey, "It's actually not all that complicated, to be honest."

"I find that incredibly hard to believe," he said, wrapping his hand around the mug. "Your best friend is marrying your ex-boyfriend. There has to be some complication there."

She shrugged, giving a smile that didn't reach her eyes. "My ex's name is Seth, and we dated from the time I was fifteen until right before college."

"I take it you broke up when you went to school?" Grey asked, then sipped his piping-hot coffee, appreciating the touches of hazelnut.

She nodded. "You know, it was funny at that time, but when I moved to Seattle..."

"Sorry," he interjected, needing to fill in the missing pieces of her life in case anyone asked him. "Where did you live before Seattle?"

"Grand Rapids." She picked up her coffee again, taking another small sip before addressing him. "I decided on Seattle for schooling, and Seth wanted to stay in Michigan."

"You didn't want to do the long-distance thing?"

She shook her head, hugging her hands around her mug as the plane bounced with the turbulence. "We thought it would make things complicated. But you know"—she paused, her gaze darkening, lost in a memory—"I hadn't thought it was a deal breaker for us at the time either."

That darkness in her eyes, that pain...Grey didn't like it. "What do you mean?"

She blinked, washing away any hint that talking about this brought up painful memories. "I mean, I figured we'd take some time for ourselves, finish schooling and all that jazz, and then I'd move home and marry him."

"You were that sure about him?"

She inclined her head. "I was that sure about him."

Even though Grey came from a happy home, where his mother and father had had an incredible marriage before his father passed away, he'd never pictured himself as a one-woman man. Marriage was an endgame, and he'd never wanted to take part in that with anyone. "So, then, what happened?" he asked, placing his coffee cup on the table in front of him.

She glanced at her coffee mug, drawing in a long, deep breath, obviously steadying herself for the conversation ahead. "It was the Christmas before I was supposed to move home. That winter was bad and, God, I remember how pretty Grand Rapids was then. All the ice and snow...it was a perfect winter." Suddenly, she laughed quietly and looked at him, eyes haunted. "I guess those aren't the details you wanted to know."

"Actually, I do want to hear those details," he corrected. "It tells me a lot about you."

She gave him a quizzical look. "What could it possibly tell you?"

It tells me everything… "That in an obviously dark memory, you're still able to see the beauty in life."

She stared at him for a long time, looking at him, completely unguarded. "You know, I never really thought of it like that, but it was a dark time. A very dark time in my life."

Grey forced his hand not to clench into a fist, an odd burn to protect her overwhelming him. "Did you find them in bed together?" he guessed.

She smiled softly. "My face is that easy to read, huh?" She picked up her coffee, and he noticed the shake in her hand when she raised the coffee cup to her mouth.

After a long sip, she continued. "I went over to my best friend Holly's house to surprise her. You see, we've been friends since we were seven years old. We were as close as two friends could be, and my going to a different college really hurt her. So I wanted to make it up to her over the holidays." Her eyes went distant again; voice took on a chilly tone. "I didn't tell anyone that I was coming home. So, I went there, opened her door, and there they were…"

"I take it you lost it?" Grey asked, knowing he would have.

She snorted softly, shaking her head. "I think I was too shocked at the time to do much of anything. I stood there while they scrambled to get their clothes on. And then after…well…how could I hate them?"

Grey's brows rose. "How. Could. You. Hate. Them?"

"I left them," she said and nodded, staring at the back of the seat in front of her, misty-eyed. "They looked to each other for comfort. They told me it didn't happen on purpose. They didn't seek it out, but it just kinda…happened. They fell in love."

Grey already hated these people, and he hadn't even met them. "I take it you accepted their admission as somehow acceptable?"

"Of course, I did," she said, wiping at her eye, erasing the moisture there. "What they told me felt like the truth. We all sat and talked, and it was clear to me that they were madly in love, and I loved them. How could I hate them for being happy?"

Grey glanced up at the light above him, feeling the air conditioning blowing on his face as he gathered his thoughts. He wouldn't have been so kind to these people, but that was his opinion, and he wouldn't shove his on to her. In a small part of his mind, he could understand where she came from, even if he wholeheartedly disagreed with her.

When he looked back at her, he found her uneasy eyes on him. "Your reaction speaks of how you love," he told her. "And it is clearly without restraint. It also shows that you're fiercely loyal. That's something to be admired. But do you think it's wise to swallow your pain to appease others?"

"No, you're right, it's not wise, it's probably something every therapist would say not to do." Again, she inhaled deeply and then blew the breath out slowly. "But I choose to ignore my pain to allow them to be happy because I'm strong enough to do that."

He pondered that and then shook his head, still disagreeing. "Listen, I'm not judging, but I am wondering if they are really worth the damage to your soul?"

She paused, considered, and then half shrugged. "At the time, I thought so."

"And now?"

"Now"—she gave a soft smile devoid of any emotion—"so many

years have passed, that it no longer matters."

"It should still matter," he stated. "Once a stain on your soul, always a stain, unless you cleanse it."

"Maybe." She glanced out the window.

He let the silence settle in and took a sip of his coffee, thinking everything through, then wondered something else. "Explain something to me. If what you're telling me is true and you've accepted them being together, then why the tears? And why did you agree to my idea of making them believe you're fine and have a perfect guy of your own?"

She gave a tight smile. "I said I was okay with their relationship, but that doesn't mean it won't sting to watch their love story play out all weekend as I stand off to the side."

"Which is exactly what's unforgivable," Grey muttered.

Warmth filled her expression. "So, what are you saying? That you would have hated them?"

"I would have hated her, and she would have felt an inch tall by the time I was through with her," he said, implicitly stating his view of all this. "And I would have beat the shit out of him."

Evie cocked her head, her eyes searching his. "All because they chose to love each other and it ended up hurting me in the process? You wouldn't have been able to forgive them?"

"No, Evie," he stated firmly. "I would have never forgiven them. And I certainly wouldn't have stood up for their fucking wedding."

"Well, I guess they should be glad I am not you," she said with a laugh, obviously to lighten the mood. "Anyways, will you play nice this weekend?"

He arched a brow at her. "Do you want me to play nice?"

"I *need* you to play nice."

Skirt Chaser

"Then around them, I'll be on my absolute best behavior."

She paused, regarded him, then gave him a *look*. "Why do I get the feeling that your best behavior might not be up to my standards?"

His arched brow rose higher. "I told you I'd be nice to them, I guess you'll just have to trust me."

"Hmm."

"But, Evie," he said with a grin, "playing nice isn't really in my plans when it comes to you. As a matter of fact, *nice* is the last thing you're going to be thinking when I'm between your thighs."

35

Chapter 4

By the time they arrived in Punta Cana, it was late afternoon. Evie was relieved to hear that Grey had arranged for transportation from the airport and had a driver waiting for them. Being rich had its perks she supposed, and after a nearly six-hour flight, she was damn happy she wasn't about to be stuffed onto a bus full of people, stopping at every resort along the way until they reached their destination.

The drive had been short and uneventful. When they reached their modern resort, located on the east coast of the Dominican Republic and nestled into a secluded tropical forest, she made a beeline for the washroom, changing into a sundress instead of the jeans she'd worn on the flight while Grey checked them into their room.

When she returned from the washroom, with her bright yellow Kate Spade purse in her hand, she found that Grey had changed, too. Now wearing a white cotton T-shirt and beige shorts with flip-flops on his feet, he looked so unlike the man she'd known while working with him. "You know," she told him with a smile, "vacation life suits you."

"I'm glad you approve." He winked and then motioned his finger in a circle. "Give me a little spin."

She grabbed the ends of her dress and spun around, her sandals squeaking against the marble floor.

"Beautiful," was all he said before planting a quick kiss on her cheek. "Our bags are being delivered to our room shortly, but how about we go and have a look around while we wait."

She nodded and smiled, and he took her hand, leading her past the reception desk. She'd have to stay on her toes. It'd be easy to forget that she and Grey weren't actually together. Holding his hand didn't exactly feel unnatural or awkward. They strode beneath a thatched roof covering the lobby, but there weren't walls enclosing the main entrance. The hot breeze carried through, smelling of the ocean and the lush tropics. Sweat dripped down her spine as they walked side by side down the palm tree-lined pathway in between the pool and the rooms on the left.

Soon, they passed the main pool, where the music blasted throughout the air, and everyone in the area looked either drunk or on their way to getting there. In only a few steps, the music faded, and instead of young partygoers, there were families and a quieter atmosphere.

She smiled at the children splashing around in the pool. Regardless of the reasons that had brought her here, she was in paradise, the blistering sun beaming down on her, reminding her that she was no longer in Seattle. "It really is quite beautiful here," she said, glancing at Grey.

He smiled and nodded. "It is that."

She noted a change in his smile, something that made him appear more relaxed than she'd ever seen. From the first day she met Grey, he'd always seemed uptight and intense...an alpha. Today, there was something in his eyes...something soft and tender, and undeniably intriguing. Again, that surprised her.

A sudden beep had her reaching into her purse. She grabbed out her phone, took one look at the screen, and sighed. "And there goes our relaxation."

Grey chuckled. "It's from Holly, I take it?"

"It's the wedding itinerary." She gave him a quick glance, and when he gave her a bored, flat look, she studied her screen again.

Wedding Weekend Itinerary
Friday, June 5th
7:00 p.m.: Rehearsal
8:00 p.m.: Rehearsal Dinner

Saturday, June 6th
9:00 a.m.: Breakfast
1:00 p.m.: Bridal Party Lunch & Spa Day
2:00 p.m.: Groomsmen's Golf

Sunday, June 7th
3:00 p.m.: Seth & Holly Tie the Knot

"Looks like we have a busy weekend ahead of us," Evie finally said, looking up at Grey again while stuffing her phone back into her bag.

Grey tossed an arm over her shoulders, starting to walk again. "We're in paradise. I'm sure we can make the most of it."

The sly way he said the latter told her that he intended to make sure of it. She couldn't fight back the heat scorching through her. Maybe that was Grey's power over women. He had this innate ability to reach down into what made a woman sensually awaken and tap into it, unleashing her desire. Hell, maybe that's why he didn't have long-term relations. This intense chemistry was the very thing he fed on.

Before she could figure out if she were on to something, a high-pitched scream blasted through the air. "Evie!"

Holly, a blond-haired beauty with big, round, blue eyes and freckles spattering her nose rushed forward. "Oh, my God, you're here." Not a second later, Evie was surrounded by Holly's flowery-scented perfume, wrapped tightly in her arms. "Can you believe how amazing this place is? It's like all my dreams are coming true."

"They totally are," Evie said, returning the hug. Back in the day, Holly was that teenage girl who had a box under her bed filled with all her ideas for her future wedding, right down to what shoes she'd wear.

After a good hard squeeze, Holly backed away and gave her classic beaming smile. Evie felt the touch of love slide through. Sure, she had friends in Seattle, but no one knew her like Holly did. They had so much history between them, it was like no time had passed since Evie had last seen her. A small part of Evie relaxed, realizing that her worries were for nothing. Evie returned the smile, realizing for the first time that she'd moved on from the past. She'd thought it might hurt to see Holly, but nothing about seeing her childhood friend hurt. In fact, Holly felt like home.

Within mere seconds, Holly's bright eyes slid to Grey. She offered her hand. "You must be the surprise guest that Evie told me about last night."

"Yes, that's right, I'm Greyson Crawford," Grey added with a voice so seductive it even rose goose bumps on Evie's arms. "You, however, can call me Grey." He took Holly's hand and kissed the top, keeping those devilishly sexy eyes on her. "Thank you for allowing me to join

Evie."

Holly giggled, her cheeks flushing pink. "Oh, of course, any boyfriend of Evie's is a friend of mine." She pulled back her hand and grinned at Evie now. "Besides, I'm just so happy to hear that Evie is dating again. She didn't exactly mention you, which was why you coming here was a bit of a surprise."

"You know our Evie here, she's too polite to be a bother," Grey smoothly said, causing Holly's smile to widen. "But I wouldn't take no for an answer."

"Well, I'm glad you didn't," Holly said and then spun around and called, "Seth, look, Evie's here."

When Evie spotted Seth turning around to face Holly, her heart leapt up into her throat. The anger towards Holly and Seth might be gone, but Evie's heart still reacted to the boy she'd once deeply loved. He was her first boyfriend, first lover, first *everything*.

Evie swallowed back the sudden emotion while Seth slowly approached as if he had all the time in the world. Tall and lean, Seth was, and always had been, the cute guy every girl wanted.

"I admit, she appears to love you," Grey said softly into Evie's ear, dragging Evie away from Seth.

"I told you they weren't horrible people," Evie whispered.

Grey's eyes stayed glued to Seth, watching his every step, but then he glanced down at Evie and gave an easy smile. "I'm not convinced of that yet."

Right as Seth reached them, he regarded Evie first. He had warm brown eyes that were so easy to get lost in, and a cute dimple when he smiled. His hair was cut short on the sides and spiked up top, but a little on the messier side than when she'd been with him. "Hi, Evie," he said.

"Hi." She smiled, and Grey slid a possessive arm over her shoulders.

Silence fell over them. Evie nibbled her lip, watching men do their sizing-up thing by staring each other down. While Seth was standing a bit taller, Grey was, in fact, taller than Seth by an inch, though his posture was relaxed, hand dangling over Evie's shoulder.

"Congratulations are in order," Grey finally said, breaking the awkward silence. "It looks like you've got the setup for quite a beautiful wedding." He offered Seth his hand. "Greyson Crawford."

Seth returned the handshake. "Good to meet you. Seth Atkinson."

Even Evie noticed the handshake seemed a little firmer than necessary, and she gave a nervous laugh.

"So, now that we're done with introductions," Holly said, sliding her arm into Seth's. "I need to know all the details since Evie's been so tight-lipped about you. How did you guys meet?"

While Evie could've gone into some elaborate story, she figured sticking as close to the truth made sense. "Grey contracted me to design the interior of one of his new high-rises."

That grabbed Seth's attention. "You're a developer?" he asked Grey.

"An architect, actually," Grey replied, sliding his fingers gingerly over Evie's shoulder, and she shivered with the rising goose bumps.

Seth's eyes narrowed slightly, and for that Evie was grateful. Now, more than ever, she realized that having Grey here, during this moment in her life that could have been emotionally taxing in every way, was a spectacular idea. She wasn't the third wheel. It was about them, not *her*.

For that, she'd always be grateful to Grey. She leaned into him, hoping he could tell that she appreciated him. "You should see the work he's done in Seattle," she said honestly, not stretching the truth here. "It's stunning. He's very talented."

Grey's mouth twitched. "Ah, angel, believe me, my work only shines because of you."

Act or no, his flattery brought out her smile.

"Awwww," Holly said, leaning her head against Seth's arm, smiling from ear-to-ear. "You guys are so cute."

Seth cleared his throat, ran a hand through his hair. "Well, ah, I should probably go and meet my family." He reached into his pocket, taking out his cell phone, glancing at his screen. "Yeah, they'll be here soon. I need to meet them in the lobby."

"Oh, yes, right, back to wedding stuff," Holly said, dropping a quick kiss on Seth's mouth and then sliding her arm into Evie's. "If it's all right, Grey, I need to take your sweet Evie here to the seamstress to make any last-minute fitting changes to her dress."

Evie doubted she'd need them. She'd sent all her measurements to Holly right after she got engaged, and her weight hadn't changed that much in a year.

"I don't mind at all," Grey said, slowly dropping his arm from Evie's shoulder. "I'm sure the bags have arrived at the room anyway, so I'll get us settled in while you go off and do your lady things." He set his gaze on Holly next, giving her those sensual eyes of his. "Bring her back to me soon, all right?"

"I'll do my best to have her back in a jiffy." Holly giggled, clearly affected by Grey's charm.

Hell, even Evie was affected right down to her bones. She stared into the warmth of his smoky eyes, heat pooling low in her body, her breath hitching. The way he commanded her with a single look was staggering. It made her want to see what he looked like aroused. And get to all the *not nice* things he'd promised.

Holly went to stride away, keeping her arm gently tucked in Evie's.

"Not just yet," Grey murmured, snatching up Evie's hand and tugging her into him. "I can't ignore that look, angel."

Like no one else was around, he sealed his mouth across hers. His hands came to her face, holding her tightly, his fingers slowly moving to tangle in her hair. His lips were soft and teasing…until they weren't. He angled her head, deepening the kiss. Her knees went weak, her body went limp, and she became hot and wet in all the right places.

When she moved closer, needing more, he sensually chuckled and backed away. "Enjoy the dress fitting, Evie. I'll see you later."

She reopened her eyes and slowly exhaled the breath she'd been holding, watching his back as he walked away.

"Good Lord," Holly exclaimed, sliding her arm into Evie's again. "You two have some serious chemistry going on. You said you found him at work?"

Evie finally blinked and managed, "Actually, I think it would be more accurate to say that he found me."

"How sweet is that?" Holly said with a whimsical sigh. "Isn't that sweet, Seth?"

Seth nodded, eyes on his phone. "Ah, yeah, I gotta get to the lobby." He leaned in and kissed Holly's cheek. "Text me when you're done with the fitting." His gaze slid to Evie. "See ya later."

"Bye." Evie smiled.

While Seth turned left on the path, heading back to the lobby, Holly and she began strolling the opposite way.

"All right," Holly said, waggling her eyebrows. "Now that we're alone, I can officially tell you how gorgeous Grey is."

Evie laughed and nodded. "He is that." With the heat he'd created still burning up her body, she wanted nothing more than to get this show on the road. "Do we have anything before or after the rehearsal later tonight?"

Holly drew in a deep breath before addressing Evie again. "Okay, so after the fitting, we're going to meet up with my family for a drink at five, if that's okay? My cousins and parents are dying to see you."

"That's cool," Evie said, "And then after that?"

"Nothing until the rehearsal at seven o'clock."

Evie smiled. *Then sex.*

A LITTLE LESS than two hours later, after Grey had ventured out to see more of the resort and enjoy a couple of beers at the bar while watching the football game on the big screen, he finished hanging his suits in the closet when Evie returned to the room. He couldn't help but smile at the heat still lingering in her eyes. Heat that he'd planted there purposely, hoping it would only grow as they were apart, her mind imagining all the things he planned to do to her.

He was glad to see that his plan had worked nicely.

The second the door shut behind her, she frowned, scanning the large, lavishly decorated, modern living room with bedroom and walk-in closet to the left, while the marble bathroom was to the right. "This is not part of the block of rooms that Holly put on hold for the wedding," she stated.

"Yes, I know," he said lightly, hoping she wouldn't be as annoyed as the first-class plane ticket had made her. "When I arranged to be added to your room yesterday, I upgraded us. I thought we deserved something a little nicer for our weekend."

She took another quick look around the room, not bothering to hide her surprised expression at the luxury surrounding her. He'd chosen one of the nicest suites. Yesterday during his search of the resort on the internet, he'd looked at the photos of the honeymoon suite first, but the room, while nicer than the standard rooms, wasn't suitable for his plans for Evie this weekend. And the presidential suite was available for their stay.

She finally sighed and looked at him again. "Do I even want to know how much this room cost you?"

He regarded her carefully, assessing her mood. "Will you object to staying here if it cost more than you think I should pay?"

"Yes."

He turned away, taking his shoes out of his suitcase. "Perhaps it's best not to tell you then."

"Grey," she said, sternly enough that it warranted a look back at her. "You don't need to do all this for me." She waved out to the room.

"This is the lifestyle I'm used to, Evie," he told her, dangling his shoes off his finger as he gave his speech. "It has nothing to do with you or using my money to *buy* you. I have the means to stay in this room, and I would even if I were vacationing alone."

She watched him with skepticism but eventually gave up with a slight shrug. "Well, I can't say it's not gorgeous." She moved to the balcony and stepped outside. "Holy shit," she called a few seconds later. "Have you seen the view of the beach from here?"

He chuckled and entered the closet to place his shoes beneath his suits. While he hadn't done this *to* impress her, he didn't mind that it did. When he reentered the room, he found that she'd placed her suitcase on the king-size bed next to his. He watched her, curious about what drove an obviously strong and sweet woman to support people who'd betrayed her. Was her heart broken? Did it make her unable to see them for the dipshits they were?

Determined to learn more about this woman, he leaned his shoulder against the wall, watching her opening her suitcase. "Can you indulge me in a little Q and A?" he asked.

"Maybe." She flipped the lid of her suitcase open.

"Are you still in love with Seth?"

Her eyes snapped to his, guarded. "Why do you ask?"

"I need to know what I'm dealing with here," he said simply.

She stared at him, pondered, and then obviously decided she trusted him enough to tell him the truth. "The young version of me still loves him, and always will. Seth was a part of my life for a long time. All my memories from my teenage years have him in them."

"What about now?" This, he needed to know.

She gave him a smile, crinkling her eyes. "I'm not that young girl anymore." With her point made, she moved past him, dresses in hand, and entered the closet.

He stayed put and called out to her, "If that's the case, then why are you here to see them get married?"

"That's a complicated answer," she called from the closet.

"Make it uncomplicated."

"I wish I could, but it *is* entirely convoluted." She exited, grabbed all her high-heeled shoes, and returned to the closet.

"All right," he said, not ready to give up just yet, desperate to understand this about her. "Tell me this, then: why in the hell haven't you ever told them that their being together hurts you?"

"First," she said, exiting the closet and returning to her suitcase. "I'm not hurt about them being together. Upset a little, but not angry, at least not anymore."

He frowned, not understanding. "There's a difference between upset and hurt?" Women were so complicated.

She placed her overnight bag on the bed, and that's when Grey noticed the sexy nature of what was in her suitcase. He withheld his smile, not wanting her to see how much her lingerie pleased him. She'd gone to a lot of effort to look pretty for him for this weekend, and he appreciated that.

"Of course, there's a difference," she said, forcing his attention back to her. She picked up said lacy items and placed them in one of the empty drawers of the dresser near the closet. "Hurt is broken. Upset is bothered."

Good and all, but something didn't add up. "If you're simply bothered by their relationship, then explain to me why you cried when Holly sent you the picture of her here at the beach?"

She shut the drawer of the dresser then turned to face him, expression hard. "Our deal doesn't mean we need to cross emotional lines, and *that* really isn't any of your business."

He grinned, loving the fight in her. In a world of women who would give him anything he wanted, here was this fiery woman who made him work for it. He liked that about her. "Fair enough," he said, switching strategies, "but answer me this: why did you come here to witness their marriage, knowing it would be hard for you?"

"Because I won't let them change me," she said matter-of-factly, placing her hands on her hips. "I was a good person before them and loved hard, deeply, and honestly, and I'll be that same person after them."

He liked that about her, too; however… "But they are not good people."

Suddenly, her expression changed, a sly smile crossing her face. "You know, for a guy that's said not to be the one-woman type, you sure are protective."

She'd meant it as a joke, but he felt that defensive heat flare through him. No matter how many lovers he had, he'd never purposely hurt a woman, nor would he ever. His rules had always been clear, not allowing for any misunderstandings.

"Protect you?" he repeated with an arched brow. "No, angel, I'm here to support you." He took the few steps forward to close the distance, and he watched her lips part and cheeks turn pink when he took her chin in his hand, forcing her lust-filled eyes to meet his. "Let me be clear," he stated firmly. "If you were mine, truly *mine*, and I wanted to protect you, the last place you'd be is here surrounded by these fucking horrible people."

She rolled her eyes yet didn't move away from his touch. "You think they're horrible people, but I'm telling you, Grey, they're not. Both Seth and Holly are kind, unique in their own ways, and I know they both care about me."

Grey's arched brow rose higher. "I think we're going to have to disagree on that fact."

Her eyes searched his, and whatever she saw in his expression softened hers, showing how tired and stressed she was. "It's just three days. That's it. Three days of…"

"Wretched people," he finished.

She laughed softly, the mirth warming her eyes again. "No, it's three days of feeling a little emotionally exhausted, then I go back to my life, and they go on to live theirs. I mean, really, before they got engaged, I hadn't seen either of them in years. Yes, Holly and I talk all the time on the phone, but after I moved to Seattle, and throughout the years, life got in the way, and we never had the time to see each other. So, I do this *for* them this weekend, and then life returns to the place where I don't have to watch them being happy."

He kept her face in his hands, unable to let her go. While, yes, he felt the desire to protect her. Evie was strong and clever, and she didn't need him to. "And that's good enough for you?"

She nodded. "It has to be."

He watched her, trying to understand her position in all this. Sure, he got that she was a good person, and wanted to be the type of woman that did decent things so good things came back to her. But being on the outside looking in, he'd be tempted to say that she was far more brokenhearted than she knew. And that all of this, her even coming here to the wedding, came from a pain somewhere deep inside her where she felt like she owed these two people something, not the other way around.

He also reminded himself that he wasn't there to help her emotionally. That wasn't the deal they'd made. He was there because he wanted to fuck this stunning creature. And maybe that purpose solidified even more now.

"Well, then, from the way I see it," he said, sliding his thumbs across her cheeks. "It's a good thing I'm here, not only to play the part of the boyfriend but also to put a damn smile on that pretty face of yours."

Her breath hitched, pupils dilated, and he loved how easily he got to her. It tempted him to see how hot he could make her. He dragged his finger across her lips and enjoyed how she stayed there, patiently awaiting his next move.

"Remind me of the itinerary plans for this evening," he said.

She licked her lips, voice breathy. "I have the rehearsal in a little less than an hour, and then we've got a dinner to attend at eight."

"A little less than an hour of free time, hmmm…" He lowered his hands to her hips and gently pushed, sending her backward until her back pressed against the wall. She gasped a little, a beautiful sound he intended to make louder.

"Why?" she asked.

He firmly dragged his finger across her bottom lip, consumed by her pretty mouth and how touching her like *this* was a total *on* button for her. "Because I've been promised something, and I'd like to claim a taste of it now." He slid his hand to her neck and ordered, "Spread your legs for me, Evie."

Chapter 5

Kisses are meant to be hot and potent and to sweep you away, but Grey's kisses were so much more. They made time stop and thoughts disappear. His fingers tightened in Evie's hair, and he cocked her head, deepening the kiss, demanding more of her mouth. She gave him all the control, melting into his touch.

A low groan rumbled from deep in his throat. He gave a final swirl of his tongue against hers and then backed away. Pinned between the wall and his hand on her neck, trapped by his smoky eyes that slowly stripped her bare emotionally with each second that ticked by, she lost herself, tumbling into where he wanted to take her. Her chest rose and fell with her heavy breaths. Her limbs began to tremble as he studied her, sensually building heat between them all with a simple look and an attitude…*his passion.*

He gave her that powerful grin, telling her he knew how crazy he made her and that he liked it. Under his potent stare, his hand came to her chin, and he leaned in, sucking her bottom lip into his mouth then giving it a gentle nibble. This kiss was different than any before it.

More experienced, maybe. More playful, even.

Keeping her locked in his hold, taking his time, kissing her chin, her neck, her earlobe, she shifted from foot to foot, outright quivering from his teasing. "Grey," she heard herself whisper, not recognizing the desperation in her voice.

He grunted, a masculine sound of pure satisfaction, and leaned away. "I like how you sounded right then." He said it like a statement, letting her know her desperation pleased him.

Mental note: be desperate more often. Because that made him act, giving her what she wanted. Him.

She held her breath, watching him lower to one knee. Feeling the quiver of anticipation deep in her belly, she swallowed the building saliva in her mouth, pressing her hands against the wall behind her.

He gathered up her skirt, grinning at her. "Hold this for me, angel."

Her fingers trembled when she reached for the thin fabric, holding her skirt up above her hips, exposing her white lace panties.

The side of his mouth curved. "I like the way you're trembling, Evie." He kissed the top of her thigh, running his hands slowly up her legs, tucking his fingers into her panties. Boldly, and with his simmering eyes still on hers, teeth nibbling his bottom lip, he slowly pulled her panties down until she could step out of them.

God, the confidence, the heat, the hunger…her heart banged against her chest, lost to everything that Grey stood for in that moment. Somehow, within his intense gaze, she felt stronger, less shy, freer. He wasn't thinking of his pleasure now, she could tell. He desired *her.* The longing she saw as he stared back at her, the knowledge that'd he been wanting and waiting to taste her, brought a ravenous hunger she couldn't ignore.

"Do not stop looking at me," he murmured, sliding his hands up her thighs.

With his big, strong hand, he gently reached for her leg, hooking it over his shoulder. Spread wide for him, vulnerable, she simply didn't have the mind space to think about all the things that might make her nervous. Not when he blew across her sex, and she shivered as he took his time.

Painfully slow, his tongue slid up her inner thigh and then moved over to the other thigh, swirling across her flesh, tickling in the most perfect way. She leaned her head back against the wall and moaned, falling into his pleasure. He played and teased, drawing out the minutes, pooling heat in her pussy, exactly where he wanted it to go.

Though each second became more desperate. She began shaking in her high heels, unable to wait any longer. "Grey," she gasped, fisting her hands against the wall.

Only then did he concede.

Using the flat of his tongue, he licked across her folds, slowly, sweetly, raising her pleasure. She moaned at his light tonguing, her eyes rolling back in her head. Every nerve ending in her body woke beneath his touch. As if he had a switch to her body that she didn't even know existed. Something only he had the power to control.

There, pinned between the wall and his mouth, he flicked out, stroking the creases of her inner thighs, then her folds, then her entrance, but never to the source of pleasure that throbbed for his mouth.

"Grey," she shouted, threading her hands into his hair.

Even then, he waited. Not until she began gasping and quivering, taken so high that the pleasure turned into sweet agony, did he act. With a low groan, he dragged the flat of his tongue upwards to the aching bundle of nerves.

A harsh moan rushed from her mouth, goose bumps trailing over her arms. He rested his hand on her pelvis, revealing her clit from beneath its hood. She glanced down, watching him tongue her clit, gently. He wasn't rushing her, she felt that. He was guiding her to where he wanted her to go. And each and every lick, suck, and tickle on her clit that his tongue expertly teased, slowly brought her higher until he wasn't so gentle anymore.

With his head buried between her thighs, he moved a little harder, a little more intently. She forced her eyes open, needing to see him. He wasn't looking at her. This wasn't about sensually teasing her, she realized that now.

He demanded her orgasm. It belonged to him.

Dear God, if he kept doing *that*, she would come, and come in ways she'd never come before. "Don't stop," she eagerly begged. "Please. Please. Don't stop." She was close, so damn close…

He shifted his shoulder, raising her leg a little higher, and groaned against her hot sex. The vibrations tickled across her flesh, hitching her breath. And with another groan, he went harder, became more focused, more determined. He swirled his tongue over her clit in waves, and it snapped her head up as she absorbed the pleasure. That's when she caught sight of herself.

Across the room, there was a mirror on the wall. The view of Grey between her thighs, with her pinned to the wall, she saw what he saw. They were strikingly erotic, staggeringly beautiful.

A blast of heat rippled across her as his mouth sealed over her clit, and his teeth gently came around the bud, holding softly, but somehow building a pleasure that had no beginning and no end. He'd taken her so high, but when his thick finger slowly slid up inside her, soon joined by another one, she only knew the sensations he was offering her.

In the mirror, she watched her hands tighten in his hair, sliding through his gel-coated strands. She pressed his face into her sex, begging him not to stop.

He didn't.

In fact, he went even harder.

His arm moved rapidly as his fingers pumped into her, his tongue stroking her clit, his teeth creating sensations and causing her pleasure to rise. But it was *him* and *her* and this stunning view that kicked her over the edge.

With a final hard thrust of his fingers and a deep suck on her clit, she screamed and then was free falling into the pleasure that he had created and then delivered on.

Time passed while she recovered, her head still hung as she caught her breath, her leg still hooked over his shoulder. She forced her eyes open and watched him slowly remove his fingers, raising them to his mouth. He sucked them deeply, his eyes fluttering shut with the pleasure of her taste.

He remained silent when he reached for her panties, and she gripped the table next to her, so as not to fall over as she stepped back into them. With the same power he exuded when he dropped to his knee, he rose.

"Kiss me," was all he said.

She smiled and raised her hands to his face, thanking him with her mouth for what he'd given her. She smelled her scent on his lips as he kissed her, not with the passion he had, but almost with gratitude as if she'd somehow given him a gift.

Within that, something was born that was unexplainable but there. A tight bond between them that connected her to Grey in ways no man had demanded before. It might have been invisible, but the strength of the connection was more powerful than anything she'd ever felt before.

He gave her a final peck on the lips, then leaned away. She smiled at him, and he smiled in return. "There's that pretty smile I like so much."

She laughed easily, feeling all the tension that had been there before now gone. "It appears you're very good at making a woman smile."

"That should not come as any surprise," he said in that strong tone belonging to him. "But you, however, have surprised me."

"I surprised *you?*" she repeated.

"Greatly, in fact," he said with a sly grin. "There's a very filthy woman inside this sweet little body screaming to get out."

Her cheeks warmed, eyes cast downward. "Don't be silly."

"Oh, I am being anything but silly." He reached for her chin, lifting her gaze to his, and one of his eyebrows slowly arched. "You like to watch."

Her gaze fell on the mirror over his shoulder, reminding her how turned on the sight of them had made her. It was a revelation that surprised even her.

She cleared her throat. "Well, I…"

"You don't need to say a thing," he said, stroking his thumb over her heated face. "Believe me, Evie, by the end of our time together, that gorgeous flush of your cheeks will be because of desire, not embarrassment about how you like to get fucked."

She gaped at him.

He chuckled, low and deep, before turning away and adding,

"Now, you have an event to go to. You'd better be on your way."

She should've left and said nothing, but in the haze of her pleasure, maybe her mind didn't have the same barriers it usually did because she found herself saying, "When are you going to take something for yourself?"

He stopped, turned back to her. "I did get what I wanted, Evie. You came against my tongue."

Again, he began walking toward the bathroom. She needed to understand his game. "But when will you come?"

"When your eyes beg me for it," was all he said before the shower turned on.

Chapter 6

Minutes before eight o'clock in the evening, Grey reached for Evie's hand, walking side by side down the stone pathway leading to the restaurant. Dressed in a flowy, white sundress and sandals that laced up her toned calves, with her hair pulled into a side braid, he was tempted to skip dinner altogether and see what those sandals looked like dangling over his shoulders.

They strode beneath the palm trees lining the pathway, and he let the silence fall between them. She radiated satisfaction mixed with hints of desire for more. He understood why her mind kept circling back to lust, he felt it, too. His cock remained semi-hard from their earlier interlude. His nostrils remembered her scent. His mouth recalled her taste. But no matter how much he wanted to drive himself deep inside her, he would wait until she *craved* him. That was the high for him, when a woman wasn't only seeking to satisfy her needs but was desperate for his touch. She was nearly there, and he planned to enjoy every moment of watching her inch higher and higher toward total surrender.

"What are you smiling about?"

Grey blinked out of his thoughts. He glanced down into her smoldering eyes, gazing upon her pinkish cheeks, and he chuckled softly. "I like seeing you this way," he admitted.

"What way?" she asked with raised brows.

"Wanting me." The widening of her eyes only heightened the desire in their depths. "It's a nice change from when you were at work and had completely shut me out."

She laughed softly, glancing back out ahead of her. "Well, I am a professional, you know."

"Yes, angel, you are." He liked this side of her, however. The uninhibited version of her. A little more relaxed, happier, maybe even freer. "Believe me, so am I, but I do have to admit it's nice not to worry about sexual harassment lawsuits," he joked.

"It is that," she said, laughing.

A couple of steps later, when they reached the Italian restaurant edging the beach, instead of going inside, he tugged on her arm, pulling her close. He folded her arms behind her back, lacing his fingers with hers. Right there to keep the heat burning between them, he sealed his mouth across hers, and he kissed her properly until he felt her soften beneath his touch.

"You asked why I was smiling. It's because of *this*." He dragged his finger across her bottom lip, something he couldn't stop from doing. It was the way her eyes burned with lust in response. Every damn time. "It's the way you react to me. It's incredibly sexy."

She pressed her lips against his thumb then smiled. "You make it easy to want you."

"Well, I'm damn glad for it, then." He chuckled, taking her hand, guiding her through the door, knowing she had maid of honor duties to attend to. He didn't want to make her late.

The second the door shut behind them, Holly called, "Evie, over here."

A quick look to the right showed Holly hurrying toward them, easing her way through the white linen-covered tables scattered throughout the candlelit restaurant.

"I didn't get to tell you at the rehearsal, but I love that dress on you," Holly said when she reached her, taking Evie into a tight hug.

Grey watched the exchange, trying to get a better sense of Holly. By all appearances, Holly seemed like a kind, upbeat, loving friend to Evie. But what kind of friend would do what Holly did to Evie? Grey didn't understand their relationship. Though he couldn't discount that might be because he usually didn't understand women in general.

When Holly stepped back, she gave Evie a very thorough once-over then repeated the gesture to Grey. "Seriously, you two make such a gorgeous couple," she said, hands on her hips. "It's enough to make anyone barf."

Evie chuckled. "Grey is pretty."

"I. Am. Not. Pretty," he retorted harshly, causing another round of laughter.

"Fine," Evie said, wrapping her arms around one of his. "Handsome. Sexy. Total stud. Is that better?"

He nodded firmly. "Much."

When he glanced back at Holly, she smiled from ear-to-ear. "Honestly, though, you both look so happy. I've never seen Evie like this before." She squinted her eyes, regarding Evie intently. "She's all lit up inside, and that makes me happy because Evie deserves all the happiness."

Evie glanced at Grey with a knowing look, to which he chuckled. All right, maybe Holly wasn't the spawn of Satan. He turned to Holly and gave her a genuine smile. "I will endeavor to keep that light lit."

"Good," Holly said with a nod. "So, enough of that." She folded her arms over her light blue sundress. "I have a question to ask you, Grey. Don't feel like you have to say yes, but—"

"What's the question?" he interjected.

"One of Seth's groomsmen got heatstroke on their fishing trip today, so they need someone to fill his spot on the golf trip tomorrow."

This is a bad idea. Instead of saying that, he glanced at Evie and sighed at her pleading expression. "Of course, I would love to go," he said, glancing back at a gleaming Holly.

"Awesome," she all but bounced. "Let me go tell Seth. He'll be so pleased."

"Can you golf?" Evie asked with a smirk, while Grey led them to the table. "We don't want you to be embarrassed out on the course."

When he reached the table where a dozen people he didn't know sat, but whom he assumed were Holly's and Seth's friends and family, he tugged her against his chest, earning wide eyes and a delicious gasp. "I would think you would know by now that I'm good at everything I do."

Her gaze flashed red-hot, but he didn't get to appreciate the heat nearly long enough because Holly said, "Come on, lovebirds. We saved you a seat at our table."

Evie stepped back, and Grey sighed against the strain of his cock. Soon, he'd have Evie in all the ways he wanted her, and that time couldn't come quickly enough. His gaze slid to the table where he noticed Seth watching Evie approach. There was something in the way Seth watched her. Something that caused Grey's back to stiffen as a man.

Seth finally glanced away, talking to a woman who seemed to be in her early fifties next to him, likely his mother, and Grey grabbed the chair, pulling it out for Evie.

When she took a seat, a soft voice said, "A gentleman. Now that is a rare find these days."

"Violet," Evie gasped, obvious elation in her expression. She shot up from her seat, and Grey stepped out of the way, watching Evie embrace the woman clearly of importance to her.

The hug lasted long enough to declare a deep love between them. When Evie backed away, a beaming smile on her face, she introduced them. "Grey Crawford, this is Violet Atkinson, Seth's grandmother."

Grey smiled at the short, stocky woman he guessed was in her early seventies, but she held quite the regal air. Her wrinkled eyes were soft and blue, and there wasn't a strand of her short, sliver hair out of place. "It's my pleasure," he told her, offering his hand. "I'm the boyfriend."

Violet smiled, returning the handshake. "A very nice-looking boyfriend, too."

Evie laughed. "I see you haven't changed at all, Violet."

Grey cocked his head, noticing the warmth in Evie's expression. He realized this was what Evie looked like with all her guards down. Curious now over her relationship with Violet, he slid out the seat he was meant to take, offering it up to Violet instead. "Why don't you sit next to Evie so you can catch up."

"Thank you, dear," Violet said, pressing her fingers with their purple fingernail polish against the table and rising from her seat.

Once she sat again, he helped her scoot her chair under the table, and then held the chair as Evie returned to her seat.

She smiled in thanks at him, and he took his seat next to Violet. Evie was wholly focused on Seth's grandmother, taking one of the woman's hands into both of hers. "I wasn't expecting you to be here."

"Why?" Violet asked blandly. "Did you think I'd be dead?"

"Oh, my God, no." Evie snickered, her eyes twinkling. "I thought you wouldn't be here because you hate flying."

"Yes, well"—she gestured across the table to Holly and Seth—"those two over there didn't give me any choice since they decided on a destination wedding."

The way she said the latter with a bit of a bite told Grey there was history there, and he got the distinct feeling that Violet liked Evie more than her grandson, and *that* he could relate to.

Violet added with a proper smile, "So, it was either be the worst grandmother in history or drink myself silly before the flight." She winked at Grey. "Which called for a nap, and is the reason for my tardiness."

Grey chuckled, reaching for his napkin and placing it on his lap.

"But you, dear," Violet said to Evie, with a soft voice and a pat on Evie's hand. "You are not someone I expected to see here. I didn't believe it when they said you'd be the maid of honor." She hesitated and studied Evie's face. "You don't look drunk at all."

"That's because I'm not," Evie said.

Violet blinked, surprise widening her eyes. "You came here willingly?"

"See," Grey interjected gently. "I'm not alone in questioning your sanity."

"My sanity is just fine," Evie rebuked, giving Grey a *look* before smiling softly at Violet. "Of course, I would be here."

"I don't understand why," Violet countered. "You know I was always on your side with all this, Evie." She drew in a deep breath before addressing Evie again. "But I figure someday Seth may be the one who oversees what retirement home I go to. So, here I am, playing the part of the nice and sweet grandmother."

God, Grey liked this woman. She reminded him of his mother.

He took a sip of his water as Violet continued, keeping her voice soft and the conversation private. "You, however, have no reason to subject yourself to this hell, my dear. Why are you here?"

A question Grey couldn't stop asking himself. Evie was smart and clever and proud, she didn't need these people in her life. But only Evie could answer that, and while she'd given a reason, Grey wasn't sure he believed it.

Evie's lips parted and then shut again. She let out a long sigh and shrugged. Maybe she was growing tired of having to explain herself.

Softness crossed Violet's expression. "Well, there is only one thing to do in times like these." She turned to Grey, waving him on. "Mr. Crawford, Evie and I need wine."

"Of course, ma'am," Grey replied, reaching for the wine bottle in the middle of the table. Positioning it over Violet's glass first, he began pouring. "Tell me when to stop."

"Stop when it's about to overflow," she said, laughing.

Once he had all three of their glasses full, someone across the table clinked their glass. When he looked in that direction, he found Holly standing, clearly in her glory to be the center of attention.

Violet muttered to Grey, "Let's do this quickly before the main attraction starts." She lifted her glass. "To Evie, and her sweet, kind, beautiful soul."

And to that, Grey raised his glass.

—⁂—

WITH A FULL belly and an easier smile from the two *large* glasses of wine over dinner, Evie held onto Grey's hand, following behind Holly and Seth and the rest of their wedding party, which consisted of friends from high school, a couple of cousins, and Seth's younger brother, Mark. Nearing ten o'clock at night now, the older crowd headed off to bed, and even Evie felt exhaustion settle in. The sun, the wine, the earlier orgasm…the nonstop wanting of Grey. She glanced beside her, toward all that heat and passion, and Grey looked as fresh as he had that morning. "It seems you won Violet over," she told him with a smile. "I've never seen her quite so smitten before."

Grey returned the smile. "The feeling is mutual. What a fabulous woman. Has she always been so…"

"Loud?" Evie offered.

"Vivacious," Grey corrected.

Evie nodded. "For as long as I can remember, she's been pretty wonderful."

"Have you always been close, you and she?"

"Always." Evie slowed her pace, walking the pathway leading back up to the main lobby where the bar and theater were located for the resort's nighttime entertainment. "Two of my grandparents lived in Costa Rica once they retired so I never saw them. And the grandparents that lived in Michigan both died within a year of each other when

I was little, so Violet was kind of a grandmother to me." She hesitated, laughing softly. "Of course, now that you've met her, you see that she's almost too fun to be called a grandmother."

"I do see," Grey agreed. "And your parents? What of them?"

"They live in Michigan. We're incredibly close. I talk to my mother on the phone a lot."

"Do you see them often?" Grey asked, seemingly truly curious.

Evie shrugged, giving a sheepish look. "Not as much as my mother would like, but it is what it is. Traveling's expensive, and she understands that." As soon as the words left her mouth, she realized maybe Grey wouldn't. He grew up with money. It was a different kind of life than hers. "Do you see your mother a lot?"

"I do," he said with a snort, glancing out in front of him before looking at her again. "You think Violet is loud, wait until you meet Anne Crawford. The woman has no filter, and she would never tolerate not seeing me."

Evie couldn't help but wonder if maybe that was why Grey seemed so straightforward. Maybe his mom had a hand in that. "She sounds like someone I'd get along with."

"You would," Grey said simply.

As they continued to walk hand-in-hand, the music from the lobby area became louder with each step they took, and Evie became more curious about his life. "You have no siblings, right?"

Grey smirked. "And just how did you know that?"

"Because I researched you," Evie added, then shook her head at him and smiled. "And before you go and get a big head about that, don't forget that your company hired me. I needed to learn about who I worked for and what they'd want from me." She paused at his grin.

"What's the smile about?"

"It all makes sense now," he muttered.

"What makes sense?"

"I had wondered where you got your bad opinions of me," he said, arching a brow. "But now I know where—clearly from the internet."

"Google knows all."

Grey adamantly shook his head, brought her hand to his mouth, and before he pressed a kiss to the back of her palm, he said, "Google doesn't know everything."

Warmth that he seemed to bring so naturally slid across her, but was hastily interrupted when Holly said, "Come on, guys, let's get some drinks."

Evie blinked then, realizing they'd arrived at the bustling bar.

The main lobby was up the stairs, but on this floor, there was a large theater off to the left. To the right, there was a seating area with wicker chairs surrounding circular tables and a salsa band playing for the crowd, with the large bar behind them serving up fancy drinks with little umbrellas.

Before she could reply, she was in Grey's arms. The scent of citrus and man filled her senses, as Grey stated in his business voice, "Holly, I'm afraid that Evie's mine for the rest of tonight, if you don't mind."

"Of course, I don't mind. Go have fun!" Holly smirked, shaking her head. "You two seriously can't keep your hands off each other, can you?"

"Not a chance in hell," was all Grey said before taking Evie's hand, leading her onto the dance floor as the band continued playing an up-beat Latin pop song. He smiled that sly grin Evie was becoming fond of, then spun her out, bringing her back in his arms, easily guiding them into the rhythm of the song.

Evie sighed, not sure what was worse: pretending she knew how to salsa dance or dancing on a completely empty dance floor. "Are you seriously going to make me dance right here in front of everyone?" she asked.

He grinned, sliding his hand across the small of her back, holding her close. "Yes, I seriously am going to make you dance right here in front of everyone, and you're going to enjoy it."

"Oh, and why is that?"

"Because you're dancing with the hottest guy here."

She barked a loud laugh, shaking her head at him. "I can always count on you to say something arrogant." His grin widened at that, but as she glanced around, she realized he wasn't necessarily wrong either.

With his one hand on her back, his other holding hers, he guided her across the dance floor, making her look like a far better dancer than she exactly was. "Seriously, you can even salsa? Is there honestly anything you can't do?" she asked.

"No."

She snorted. "No? Really?"

"No," he repeated. "If I need to be good at something, I work hard until I am great at it, and that includes learning to dance in college since"—he winked—"women like that."

"You know," she said, starting to see that his arrogance was more just stating the truth, while he spun her out again and then brought her back in close. "I have never met anyone like you before."

"I'm glad."

She rolled her eyes, following the way his hips swayed. "And why is that?"

"It means I have no competition."

She laughed, easily…maybe even easier than she had in a long time. But then she caught the crowd staring at her…all those eyes…all those people. "I don't do this well," she grumbled, looking at him. "I'm not used to being the center of attention."

"There's nothing to do." Grey slid his thumb across her hand, lowering his voice into that rumbly tone. "Just stay here, look at me, the rest doesn't matter."

She sighed again. "But—"

"My God, Evie." Grey squeezed her hand, shaking it a little. "Is it impossible for you to stay quiet and simply enjoy something?"

Again, she sighed. "But—"

Her voice hastily cut off as he leaned down and whispered in her ear, "There will be a time when I quiet your beautiful mind."

When he straightened up, she couldn't help but play along. He made her want to. "That sounds like a promise, Grey."

"It is that, angel." He grinned.

He gave her another spin then settled into one spot as the band changed to a slow song. They stayed there, slowly swaying their hips to the beat, and she became lost in his smoky eyes. She'd come to realize that he was so different than her first impression of him. Before this trip, she thought Grey was a ladies' man on a power trip. A guy not to be trusted because he'd break her heart. Now… "I think maybe it's time I apologized."

"Apologize?" he said with raised brows. "For what?"

"For judging you wrong." He slowed his dancing, and she bared it all, knowing he deserved to hear it. "I thought you were this certain type of guy, and I treated you like you were that man. But…now I know that you're one of the most solid guys I've ever met. You came here with me to help make this wedding easier. I'm still not entirely sure what you're getting out of all this."

"I told you before," he murmured, dropping his mouth closer to her. "I get you."

"But you haven't had me yet."

He inclined his head. "Oh, but I will."

She gave a shy smile, unable to disagree with him there. He seemed to be after something before he took things to the next level, and if she were honest, she wasn't exactly sure what that was, but she could feel the tension building between them. "Take that for example. Before, I thought your boldness was arrogance. Now, I see that confidence as something else entirely."

"What do you see?"

Maybe it was the wine, being in paradise. Maybe it was him, but she spoke her truth. "I see a man who knows his worth. I see a man who demands people around him live up to those expectations. It's not haughtiness, which is what I thought it was. It's because you're good and honest and real, and you demand that people treat you with the respect you know you deserve." She drew in a deep breath before addressing him again. "I think it was hard for me to see that before."

"But now?"

"Now I want you to know that I'm sorry for the way I treated you," she continued, not letting herself cop out. "I'm sorry that I haven't said a hundred times before now that you're a good, strong man, and that all of this, everything you're doing for me, is one of the nicest things anyone has ever done."

A warm smile crossed his face as he released her hand to cup her cheeks. "Thank you for that, Evie."

In the manner that was so Grey, without caring that they had an audience, he pressed his mouth against hers. At first, his kiss was teasing. A light embrace that was as playful as it was intentional to draw her in.

A few seconds later, everything changed. His fingers tightened on her face, and his kiss became hot and demanding. He angled her head and slanted his mouth over hers, and in that second, she belonged to him.

Heat pooled between her legs, making her hot and wet and ready. Though his statement, his declaration in front of anyone watching was so much more than that. His passion consumed her. She burned like a fever, and she needed a cure, and that cure was Greyson Crawford.

He broke the rules she'd set for herself.

He freed her.

And she felt reborn in that liberty.

When he backed away, she reopened her eyes to his smoldering gaze. "Grey," was all she could think to stay, simmering with a desire she couldn't control.

"Yeah, angel, I know." He gave her a heated smile, brushing this thumb across her bottom lip, igniting the fierce burn rushing up her spine. Then he added, "It's time."

Chapter 7

Back at the room, Grey shut the door behind him then moved to the living room, leaning his shoulder against the wall, arms folded. Evie slowly approached the bed, taking her time. Silence had fallen between them on the way back to the room. It was the kind of heavy silence that spoke of her nerves. Grey grinned; she was such a sweet little thing who likely had very few one-night stands, if any. It just so happened there wasn't a nervous flutter in his gut. He'd waited one month for this moment.

To have her.

To own her.

He kept a firm eye on her as she stopped at the bench at the end of the bed, and he noted the way her shoulders moved with a deep breath. His cock swelled in his pants, all that innocence a delightful treat. He had liked this game between them over the weeks that she worked for him. This push and pull.

His patience had been worth it because he won, he saw that now. Her surrender was right there, ready for him to take. Nothing had ever felt *this* good. The high of a win, professionally or personally, had never been this rich before.

When she finally turned to face him, lacing her hands together, he broke the silence. "There are two ways we can go about this," he told her.

"What ways are those"—her mouth twitched—"missionary or on top?"

He chuckled, thinking her nervousness came out in a cute way. "No, angel," he said, approaching her. When he reached her, her spicy scent flowed around him, and he added, "Your way, or my way."

She visibly swallowed, cheeks flushing pink. "What's your way?"

"I can show you." He lifted his hand, slid his thumb up her neck, across her pounding pulse. "Do you want to see?"

"Yes," she rasped.

"Stay here." Instead of giving her the kiss he knew she craved, he moved into the closet, took out the small, brown leather bag he'd brought in his suitcase then returned to her. Intrigue filled her eyes when he put the bag down on the bench. "Open it," he told her.

She gave him a curious look then stepped forward and unzipped the bag, peering inside. Seconds later, her head slowly lifted, brows raised. "Who are you?" she asked, laughing.

He chuckled, brushing his knuckles against her cheek, loving that smile. "I like my sex to have a particular flavor."

"A filthy, dirty flavor, apparently."

He inclined his head, gesturing to the bag of sex toys. "I assume some, or all of this is new to you."

She gazed inside the bag again, slowly reaching for the blindfold and hanging it off the tip of her finger. "Except for the vibrator, I'm new to it all." She reached in again and pulled out the leather straps, giving a nervous laugh. "To be honest, these scare me a little."

"They're not for whipping you, if that's what you're worried about."

She let out a long breath, visibly relaxing. "So, you're not a sexual sadist?" At that, he arched a brow, and she snickered. "I watch *Criminal Minds*."

"Ah, I see." He took the leather strap from her, running the soft leather through her hand. "But, no, I'm not a sexual sadist. I don't get off inflicting pain, or receiving it for that matter. What I do like is kinky sex where I'm in charge. Full power exchange. Nothing I would do would ever leave a lasting mark, except maybe a slight redness to your skin that would fade within an hour or so."

"All right…" She cocked her head, regarding him closely. "How long have you been into this?"

"Since my early twenties."

She closely watched him drag the leather through his hand, eyes glistening with intrigue. "What exactly would you do with that?"

"It's easier to show you than explain."

"Well…" She nibbled her bottom lip, her eyes fixated on his hands.

To stop her nerves in their tracks, he took her chin, lifting her eyes to his. "Remember our terms, angel. You have nothing to lose here. We have this weekend." He moved closer, bringing his heat near her, loving the little shiver she gave. "We can have traditional sex, and I will be content with that, or we can give our time together an erotic flavor." Needing this to be clear, he stepped back, giving her some room to think. "What's your choice?"

Her cheeks were flushed, her pupils dilating before his eyes, and he saw her say *yes* before her mouth parted. "Yes."

Still, he needed more consent than that. In this game, misunderstandings could not happen. "We need to be clear at all times, Evie. I need to hear the words. Do you want me to use sex toys on you?"

"Yes"—her cheeks burned bright pink now—"I want you to use sex toys on me."

"Better," he said with a firm nod. "The leather straps?"

"Yes, you can use the leather straps."

"Excellent," he said, moving to the bench. He placed his bag on the floor and then sat on the bench and hooked his finger, calling her forward. Those cheeks still flushed a pretty pink when she stopped in front of him, and went even brighter when he said, "Undress for me, Evie."

She hesitated, eyes huge. "I… This is hard for me."

"I'm sure it is," he replied, "but these are my rules. I want you naked so I can play."

She exhaled a long, slow breath and then reached for the strap of her dress, slowly pulling it off. Soon, the other strap was gone, and within seconds, her dress pooled at her feet. Next, she removed her bra, slowly, teasingly. Like a predator watching his prey, he couldn't look away as her tits sprang free, her tiny, puckered nipples awaiting his mouth. She was a beauty, and once she slid her panties down, stepping out of them, she revealed her neatly shaved pussy to him again.

Before his plan was to move ahead with the leather straps to completely rid her of her nerves, but with this view, he couldn't help but reach forward and stroke her rounded stomach. She shivered beneath his hand when he ran his touch up to a heavy breast, and he massaged her. When he moved onto the next, he groaned at the feel of her. So perfect. So ready for all that he wanted.

This woman he'd craved for weeks…her being bared to him was so much more than what he imagined. But it was the sweetness in her eyes, the slight nervousness that sucked him in, weaving a spell around him that he couldn't break.

"Was I worth it?" He snapped his eyes up to her face, finding them filled with desire. She added with a shake to her voice, "What you see now…was it worth coming here with me?"

He stroked her belly and arched a brow at her. "Angel, I would have done anything and everything to look at what I'm looking at right now." Determined to move ahead, he reached for the leather strap again. "Come closer." She gave him that cute smile again and took the two steps to be right in front of him. "Spread your legs for me."

To take the spotlight off her for a little bit, he looked away from her face and smiled with her long exhale. He could intimidate, he knew that. Staying on task, he slid the leather around her left thigh and then fastened the buckle, ensuring the metal loop rested on the outside of her thigh. Once done, he reached for the other leather strap in the bag, and she shivered again when he tightened that strap around her bare thigh, nice and tight.

Leaving her there, he rose and reached back into his bag, taking out three more straps. He moved to the desk across the room, took hold of the dark wood chair, repositioning it into the center of the room where he wanted it.

When he returned to her again, he found her breathing heavily, the anticipation partly frightening, he was sure, yet exciting all the same. He couldn't fight his grin when he placed the straps on the bed, and one by one, strapped them to her upper arms, tightening until he knew they wouldn't slip off. Once done, he picked up the final strap and placed the collar around her neck, with the metal loop facing him.

Once finished with his work, he stepped back and examined her. Sweetness in bondage, a very pretty sight indeed. Her nipples were in tight buds, her breathing heavy and deep. She was so stunning, creating an infectious warmth to flow over him. So much so, he needed to be closer, and cupped her chin, sealing his mouth over hers. She easily melted into his kiss, moaning with the stroke of his tongue. He reached for her breasts, massaging both, tweaking her nipples until she wiggled with the intensity. Only when he heard that higher pitched moan, all but begging him to own her, did he back away.

"Stay there for me, angel." He moved back to the bag and took a condom from the box there as well as the black silk blindfold.

With her eyes on him, he moved to her again and slid the blindfold over her head, settling it onto her eyes, making sure not a hair was out of place. He wanted her perfect. All *his* to enjoy in the way he'd wanted to enjoy her. "I control what you see now, angel"—he dragged the tip of his finger down her arm—"and when you see it."

She moaned, and he grinned, imagining for a woman whose kink was voyeurism, this would be the best type of foreplay. It fucked with her mind, and he'd use that to his advantage tonight.

Keeping his eyes on her, a naked beauty awaiting his sin, wearing nothing but his leather squeezing her creamy flesh, and a black blindfold, she made his dreams a reality. Slowly, he removed his shirt, then his shorts, taking his boxer briefs with them. He took his time, letting anticipation build as he opened the condom and applied it to his hard cock. Then he reached back into his toy bag for the chain with the clips on the end, and rattled it for her to hear.

She cocked her head, obviously listening hard. He suspected she wondered what he planned to do to her. That thought excited him. He liked surprising her. He wanted her to think all the things her mind could dream up, because soon, she'd be honest with him and tell him her fantasies, and then he could fulfill them.

Hot and hard, he returned to her, and her breath hitched when he dragged his fingertips gently up her arm. Sliding his hand downward, he took hers and gently tugged her forward to the chair, assisting her to sit. He let the silence play out between them when he slid the chain through the loop on her neck, the arm's chair, the loop on her arm, then lifted her leg to click the end onto the loop there, binding her to the chair.

By the time he'd finished with the other leg and arm, she was spread wide open for him, perched on the edge of the seat, locked down to the chair. And all *his*.

He waited…until her cheeks flushed bright pink, telling him emotions overwhelmed her. Only then did he close in on her. He grabbed the base of his cock, using his hardened length to stroke her clit. She moaned, head tilted back against the chair, chin pointed up to the ceiling.

This…this was all for him.

He tapped her clit with the head of his cock, smacking those nerves and waking up her body for the treat he planned. When she gave him the moan he wanted, he slid his cock down through her folds, until he slipped *just* inside her. He could have drawn this out and played for hours, but she was too new, too nervous, too desperate.

Trust was earned through the first touch, and he wouldn't fuck it up. Leaving his cockhead inside her, he massaged her breasts, appreciating all of her. This view hadn't been by chance. The first time he'd dreamed of her, this was how she looked. Blindfolded and bound in his leather to a chair. Maybe she thought he was playing around, but this wasn't part of the game. He'd fantasized about her, and now, he fulfilled the fantasy that had haunted him day after day for a month.

With the thrill of that engulfing him, and the power overwhelming him that he'd conquered his latest challenge, he grabbed onto the arms of the chair and shifted his hips, slowly entering her. Her loud moan echoed his.

"Holy fuck," she breathed.

Typically, he'd reply, but right now he was consumed by her. The feel of her. The scent of her. Back and forth, her tight channel squeezed him as he worked his cock inside her. Her moans became a sound he'd never forget as he stared down at her parted mouth.

Determined that she come with him, he lowered his thumb to her clit and worked the little bud, until she began writhing beneath him, straining against the bindings. He growled, fighting off his orgasm as her inner walls convulsed around his shaft, demanding he blow. Urgency overtook him when he reached for the blindfold and had it off a second later. "Open your eyes," he ordered.

She blinked once before he turned her head, and then slowly her eyes widened. There, in the mirror, she stared at herself, bound to the chair in his leather straps, her pink lips swollen from his kisses, her cheeks flushed from the pleasure.

"Oh," she gasped. "Oh, God…." Her sex clenched, tightening like a vise against his shaft. Soft moans spilled over him.

She felt too good. She looked too pretty. Emotion he wasn't expecting overwhelmed him. Protect. Claim. Defend. All his primal instincts were on full alert. He began to pound her pussy harder, groaning against the warmth inside. His sac tightened, telling him he'd been teased too much over the past month, and the reality of her was too much to handle.

"Grey," she screamed, breaking apart around him.

With a final roar, he crashed over the edge with her, bucking and jerking his pleasure.

Sometime later, when consciousness finally returned to him, her soft chuckle brushed across him. Breathless, he lifted his head from her chest where he was all but slumped on top of her. He discovered she was resting her head back against the chair, looking boneless and perfectly well fucked. "Something to add?" he asked with an arched brow.

"Your way is *so* much better than my way," she said with twinkling, satisfied eyes.

He chuckled, pressing a soft kiss against her mouth. "You're damn right it is."

Chapter 8

The next morning, standing in front of the bathroom mirror, Evie ran a brush through her damp hair. With the spa day scheduled for an hour from now, she skipped makeup altogether for the day, figuring it was pointless to wear any.

"What time do you think you'll be back from the spa?"

She glanced into the mirror, finding Grey stepping out of the all-glass shower behind her, droplets of water sliding down his six-pack. The tattoos covering his arm looking blacker than gray. Though what drew her attention most was his semi-hard cock. They'd *just* had shower sex minutes ago, and he already wanted more of her. Grey had quite the appetite, and she supposed she liked that about him. A lot. "I'll be back before you, I'm guessing," she finally said, glancing up into his eyes, discovering them a little heated from her obvious ogling. "Probably around mid-afternoon."

"Shall I make us plans for later?" He grabbed a white bath towel off the hook and wrapped it around his waist, giving a cheeky smile. "Or do you have more maid of honor duties to attend to?"

"Actually," Evie said, placing the brush down beside her makeup bag, "later tonight, I'll be sleeping in Holly's room with her."

Grey stopped mid-movement as he tucked the towel against his hip, slowly lifting his head, frowning. "You won't be with me tonight?"

"Didn't I tell you that?"

"No, you didn't," he grumbled, obviously annoyed, and finished tucking the towel against his hip. "Though I suppose it's understandable." He thrust his hands into his hair, shaking out the excess water. "That is a wedding tradition for best friends, isn't it?"

"It is." Evie nodded with a smile, glad he understood.

"Well, then," Grey drawled, stepping closer. "I suppose I must get my fill before you leave me for the night, hmm?" Eyes on hers through the mirror, he stepped in behind her, letting her feel his rock-hard erection now. He gave a moan, causing her to shiver, and he swiped her hair off to one shoulder then tucked a finger into the strap of her sundress, slowly sliding it down. God, it was the way he looked at her...touched her...she was needy, desperate for him to take control. She held her breath, anticipating the intensity of his mouth when a sudden knock at the door cut through the heat. His low chuckle rumbled against her shoulder when he pressed a single kiss there and then moved away. "And the universe has spoken. My taste will have to come later."

Evie exhaled the breath she'd been holding, pressing her hands against the vanity. "Expecting someone?" she asked, a little breathless.

"That's our breakfast," Grey said. "Let me go get that settled." He grabbed his sport shorts, dressed, and was out the bathroom door a second later, shutting it behind him.

Evie, on the other hand, needed a minute to recover. Her body was in a perpetual state of arousal. The good thing was, at least Grey delivered on the promises he made. She considered herself in the mirror, noting the flush in her cheeks and her enlarged pupils. The man had gifts, of that she was certain.

When her stomach rumbled, reminding her she needed food to refuel, she picked up her towel from the floor, hanging it on the hook to dry. As she reached for the door handle, she heard voices coming from the other side. A long enough conversation that it didn't seem like room service.

Maybe Holly had changed her mind about meeting at the spa and came to the room to walk with Evie instead. Refocused on things other than her raging hormones, she opened the bathroom door.

"How long have you worked here?" Grey asked.

Evie stopped in the doorway, listening to an unfamiliar feminine voice with a thick Spanish accent reply, "For a few years now."

"Ah, I see," Grey said softly with a tone that Evie heard him use with her, smooth as silk, and oh-so-seductive. "And do you like this sort of work?"

"Certainly, señor, I get to meet very attractive men." The woman laughed, all too sultrily.

Evie'd had quite enough of listening to the invitation for sex practically purring from the girl's mouth. Barefoot, she padded her way into the living room, finding Grey leaning a shoulder against the wall, arms crossed. The gorgeous brunette with the stunningly tanned olive skin stood in front of him, wearing the resort's uniform of a white golf shirt and navy blue shorts. She was practically pushing her great tits out and batting her thick dark lashes at Grey.

Neither Grey nor the woman noticed Evie when Grey added, "I suppose that would be a perk to the job."

"Sí, señor." The woman smiled, giving Grey's bare chest a very thorough once-over. When she met his eyes again, she gave a sensual smile. "A very nice perk to be sure."

Evie rolled her eyes, about ready to gag. She hoped to hell she didn't look like this when Grey turned all that heat on her. It bordered the line of pathetic. She cleared her throat, intending to end whatever the hell they thought was going on here. Sure, her relationship with Grey might be a fraud, but was it necessary to throw that in her face?

When Grey glanced her way, she raised her eyebrows.

He studied her face for a moment and then gave his sly smirk before grabbing the bill off the tray with the food. He handed it to the woman. "Gracias."

"Ah, sí, you're welcome, señor." The woman accepted the bill, hiding her gaze from Evie. Obviously, she didn't know that Grey wasn't alone.

She gave Grey one last look then silently left the room, shutting the door behind her.

Grey didn't even flinch, moving to the cart and taking off the metal dome covers, revealing pancakes, fresh fruit, waffles, bacon, and sausage. "I wasn't sure what you wanted when I ordered, so I got a little of everything."

He seemed intent to move past that show. Evie couldn't. "Are you sure you don't want to go after her?" she asked.

"Why would I?" Grey asked, reaching for a piece of bacon and nibbling on the end.

Back as stiff as a pencil, Evie stated, "That girl was all over you. I can't help but wonder had I not interrupted you, would you have gotten her number and hit up the staff quarters later?"

He snorted a laugh. "Evie, that girl was twenty years old at most. She's a child."

"She was basically offering you sex on a platter."

"Yes, I know what she was offering me," he said gently, finishing off the piece of bacon. "But just because she's offering sex, doesn't mean I'll accept. I'm here with you, angel."

"For three days, Grey," Evie replied, trying to ignore the instinct telling her that his flirting was bad. "I know what the deal is."

"You're missing the point," he said, stepping closer, intensity burning in his expression. "What she was doing has nothing to do with what I was doing. Which was nothing."

Evie pushed the emotion back and back some more until logic peeked through. "You're right. God, I'm not used to this, I'm sorry."

"Sex without a relationship, you mean?"

She laughed softly, breaking the tension, hoping to end this horribly embarrassing conversation. "That, and, apparently, it's easy to forget we're not actually in a relationship, and I have absolutely no reason to be bothered when a pretty girl hits on you."

"Well," he drawled, using that sexy voice on her now, "we might not be in a relationship, but let me remind you what we are doing." He grabbed on to the front of her sundress and tugged her forward, sliding his other hand over her nape, where he held her firmly.

His sculpted mouth curved slightly. Obviously, he found her jealous streak amusing. Well, she never had to share her boyfriends. What was hers was hers until they weren't, and then it no longer mattered who they flirted with.

These thoughts held strong in her mind until he sealed his mouth across hers, burning his desire into her very core. His tongue was wicked and demanding. His strong arm wrapped around her back, pulling her in close. She may have questioned where his mind had been before but not anymore. She felt his loyalty to her this weekend in his hot kiss as he guided her along on his passionate ride.

When he broke the embrace, her breath hitched, and her lower body burned for more of his heated touch. His grin was sinfully delicious as he dragged his thumb across her damp bottom lip. "Remember, Evie, I'm here with *you*. My game. My rules. Your surrender," he murmured against her mouth. When he backed away, his expression turned playful. "Forget that again, and I'll spank that sweet bottom until you truly believe me."

"You wouldn't dare," she stated, not sure if he was serious or not.

He grinned a promise. "Try me."

LATER THAT MORNING, the sun beat down on Grey's exposed arms beneath his white golf shirt as he exited the golf shop located to the right of the clubhouse with the thatched roof and white-and-gray marble floors. While the company might not be great today, the views were spectacular. Thick, lush tropical forests surrounded the bright green eighteen-hole golf course.

"Grey, you're with me."

He drew in a deep breath, centering himself, slipping on the baseball cap that he'd bought at the golf store inside, as well as a glove, and he glanced in the direction of Seth's voice. At the bottom of the stairs, Seth waited in the golf cart with the two golf bags in the back. *This is not going to end well.*

Determined to take a bad situation and make it better, he pushed away any preconceived notions about how he thought this day might go and trotted down the stairs toward Seth.

When Grey reached him, Seth grabbed a beer can from the cooler in the back of the golf cart. "A morning refreshment?" Seth smiled, offering the beer.

"Sure." Grey accepted the frosty beer, sliding into the open passenger seat. Behind him, he noticed the rows of golf carts full of Seth's family and friends, including Seth's best man. "Your best man, what was his name again?" Grey asked.

"Jeremy," Seth said, reaching for a beer.

Grey cracked open his can, needing to ask the obvious question. "Would you not rather golf with Jeremy? I can team up with someone else."

"Nah, it's cool, don't worry about it. Jeremy's with my dad." Seth placed the can in his cup holder then hopped into the driver's seat.

With no way out of this, Grey downed a quarter of his beer, while Seth put the golf cart into drive, leading the way as the rest of his family and friends followed behind in a roar of laughter.

In this golf cart, the tension was thick and heady.

Grey leaned back in his seat and took another big gulp, preparing for the next few hours. Seth could only want Grey with him for one reason, to talk about Evie. That reason was not something Grey wanted to talk about. Not after the tension from this morning.

"Do you golf a lot?" Seth asked, making his way toward the beginning of the pathway which led to the first hole.

"Not often, I'm afraid." Grey placed his beer in the cup holder to put on his glove.

"Not much of a sports guy then?"

Was Seth sizing him up? Grey grinned. "Business comes first, always."

Seth quickly glanced away, clearly realizing that, financially, Grey's balls were bigger. He followed the bend in the path. When they passed a group of golfers, he spoke up again. "So, how serious are you and Evie?"

Grey sighed internally, reaching for his beer again and taking another sip. He knew Seth's type through and through. He wanted what he couldn't have. Grey swallowed the beer in his mouth and then arched an eyebrow. "Are you sure you want to have this conversation?"

Seth shrugged, eyes on the pathway. "Unless it's too awkward for you."

Grey grinned again at the challenge in Seth's voice. If this were any other guy, he'd have him put in his place in two-point-two seconds. Seeing that he had to play nice for Evie's sake, he kept his voice pleasant. "It's not awkward in the least. I know you two dated for a while, and I'm sure you're only looking out for her." *Bullshit!* "To answer your question, I'd say that we're serious."

"Serious enough to marry her?" Seth turned the golf cart to the right, following the bend in the pathway.

"It's not something I considered before, to be honest," he admitted, sticking to as much of the truth as he could. "But with her, I would say that I would never rule out marriage." He thought that needed to be added.

"Cool," was Seth's reply.

It wasn't a happy *cool*, it was sad and disappointed. It made Grey more curious about what in the hell this guy had been thinking when he let Evie go. "Evie told me about you two. High school sweethearts, she said."

"Yeah." Seth gave Grey a quick look and a dark smile. "We had some good times."

And I took her virginity.

Seth hadn't needed to say it; Grey saw it all over his face. A burn erupted in his chest, but he took another sip of his beer, keeping his mouth shut and washing away his irritation. *For Evie,* he reminded himself. "Young love is a very sweet thing, but can't really be compared to what loving a woman can be like."

Seth's eyes narrowed on the pathway, obviously, a nerve had been hit. Grey took a little joy in that, hastily adding, "I can only imagine that's how it feels with Holly. So different than what you had in your teens, am I right?"

"Right," Seth muttered. "Holly's pretty great."

There was something in Seth's face that raised Grey's alarms. Too tense. Too intense. Something was *off* about Seth's posture. He watched Seth closely, as he added, "She's full of spirit, for sure."

Seth scowled, grabbed his beer, and took a long sip.

Paying closer attention now, Grey noted the way Seth's hand shook, and there was tightness around the corners of Seth's eyes. Grey had seen this look on men before. Seth had ghosts following him.

Careful not to make Seth erupt, which in turn would cause trouble for Evie, Grey asked, "Any nerves about the wedding tomorrow?"

"Fuck it," Seth suddenly snapped. He stopped the golf cart on the side of the pathway and waved everyone forward.

His father, a short, stocky man with white hair, and Jeremy, a perfect Ken doll, stopped beside the cart. "Everything all right, son?" his father asked, concern in his eyes.

"Just gotta take a piss," Seth said. "Go on, we'll be there in a few."

"Be quick," his father said, oblivious to the tension Grey could feel radiating off Seth. His father waved forward. "Onwards, Jeremy."

Seth gripped the steering wheel, knuckles white.

Grey clenched his jaw muscles then took another sip of his beer, knowing what was coming. It was why he'd come with Evie; he was there to make Seth jealous. Truth be told, he hadn't expected this turn of events, but he also hadn't known the story about Evie's past with Seth until they were on the plane. When Seth turned to him, looking utterly broken, Grey knew he'd done a far better job than just making him jealous. Grey had made Evie desirable to the one man who'd discarded her.

When all the golf carts faded into the distance, Seth turned to Grey, his cheeks flushing red-hot. "Are you in love with her?"

Arching a brow at both his tone and the question, Grey stated, "That is your business because…?"

"Because I want to know," Seth said through clenched teeth.

While Grey had assumptions about what was going on here, he needed to be clear, not only for Evie but also for himself. "Do you want to know because you're looking out for Evie or because you're wondering this for yourself?"

Seth glanced away, staring off at something in the distance, but in his eyes, there was a darkness that Grey had seen before. Evie was haunting Seth; she simply didn't know it. "I haven't seen her in so long," Seth said, voice strained.

Grey heaved an even longer sigh, finishing off his beer then crunching the can in his hand. Had he been Evie's real boyfriend, Seth would've been knocked on his ass faster than he could blink. But here, seeing Seth now, Grey realized a truth. Seth had picked the wrong woman, and he knew it. "You're getting married tomorrow morning," he reminded Seth.

"Fuck, I know." Seth ran a hand across the back of his neck. "But then I saw her…" He paused, shaking his head. "So I'm asking you"—he turned to Grey, desperation in his eyes—"how serious are you?"

Grey glanced out at the golf carts off in the distance, wishing he could be on one of those and not in this cart. How would Evie want him to handle this? Would she want to know that Seth obviously still had feelings for her?

He decided on his plan quickly. Not only wasn't it his place to decide. He didn't give a fuck what Seth wanted, and he wouldn't let it rain darkness over his weekend with Evie. Seeing there was no way out of this, he faced Seth. "Depends on why you're asking. You've hurt her. I won't let you do that again." That, he meant.

Seth hung his head. "I didn't mean to hurt her. I—"

"Fell in love with her best friend."

He snapped his head up but immediately shook the glare off his face. "I suppose I deserve that. Still, you haven't answered me."

Stay the fuck away from her, echoed in Grey's mind. Though the truth was, he wasn't really dating Evie, and she could do whatever she wanted. "I am not Evie's keeper, nor am I yours. It doesn't matter how serious we are or not. Whatever you're thinking, or planning to do, is your business, not mine. And to be perfectly honest, Seth, this is a conversation that I feel you need to have with Evie, not me." Done with this shit and this asshole next to him, he gestured toward the pathway. "Your family and friends are waiting for you. You've planned a golf game for today. I suggest we play it."

It took a few seconds, but Seth finally glanced away and returned his foot to the pedal, sending the golf cart forward. "I hope since you know this is my situation to deal with," he said, "then you will leave it to me to talk about."

"My loyalty is to Evie," Grey said. "If anything could hurt her, I will tell her."

Seth paused. Then, "And what if I intend to love her?"

"Then she'll have to make a choice."

IN THE LARGE, rectangular room, with tropical jungle plants in every available space possible except for the pathway leading to the three different in-ground natural spring pools—all at different temperatures—Evie moaned, sliding into the hottest of the three pools. She moved straight for the waterfall, which wasn't only pretty to look at, but apparently, she'd been told by the lady who welcomed her into the spa, it was also hydrotherapy. When she reached the waterfall, she groaned happily. The water pounded against her shoulders, massaging the muscles with its force.

"What a waste of my time."

Recognizing that voice, Evie reopened her eyes, finding Violet stepping into the pool wearing a classic fifties-style, black bathing suit. For a woman in her early seventies, Violet sure looked good. Fit and vivacious, Evie hoped to be like her when she was that age. She exuded life, and always had, even since Evie's teens. Though she was also easily annoyed. As a woman from the South who lived a privileged life, she expected a certain kind of treatment. Apparently, she hadn't received it thus far.

Evie chuckled. "What's got you tied up in knots, Violet?"

Half swimming, half walking, Violet made her way over and said, "A lady wasted five minutes of my life telling me how beneficial these baths are."

"Perfect for cleansing the body, releasing endorphins, and for stimulating blood circulation," Evie said.

Violet smiled. "Ah, you heard the same speech."

"I did."

"There is absolutely no reason to go into all that," Violet said, waving out to the space. "When you have this to enjoy, who cares what the damn water does. This place is good for the soul. Besides, who knows how long I have left. I need all the minutes I can get for important things."

"Which are?" Evie asked.

"Not listening to the damn speech." Violet gave a little smile and dipped lower under the water. "So, I see Little Miss Center of the Universe is still getting her massage."

"Violet," Evie snapped, looking in every corner, making sure Holly's cousins weren't within hearing distance. "You shouldn't say those things about Holly. But, yes, she went in for sixty minutes, instead of the thirty we did."

"Ah, good, thirty more minutes without that boyfriend-stealing twit." Violet sighed, and Evie couldn't help but chuckle, as Violet added, "That means we have more time to ourselves. It's been so long since you've come home. This is nice, isn't it, sweetheart?"

Guilt landed like a rock in Evie's gut. Sure, she called Violet often and caught up, but a phone call wasn't like seeing the person. And she'd managed to do all her maid of honor duties remotely. "I'm sorry I haven't come to see you, it's just—"

"Hard." Violet smiled and patted Evie's arm. "I know that, and I understand, but we don't have to talk about *that*. The past is the past, there's no sense bringing up painful things. You've got this new, exciting life. Let me hear about that. You seem smitten with this Greyson Crawford."

Evie narrowed her eyes on Violet's innocent expression. "You Googled him, didn't you?"

"Of course, I did," Violet said without shame, waggling her eyebrows. "I wanted to see who captured your heart."

"Violet, that's terrible," Evie rebuked, even though she had done the same thing. Though that was different, it was for work, not to spy on him. "You shouldn't Google anyone. Who knows what you'll find on the internet."

"If Grey has nothing to hide, then it shouldn't matter what I look up," she said, chin lifted in her defense. "In case you were wondering, I found nothing uncouth. He appears to come from a wealthy family."

"He does, and no, that's not why I'm with him."

Violet smiled. "I know that, dear, but it's still a positive." She swatted at the air, water dripping from her fingers. "No more of that, tell me more about you two. I've never seen you look so"—her pale eyes searched Evie's, so wise and warm—"yes, smitten."

Evie swirled her hands in the water, her heart rate kicking up a notch. "What exactly does smitten look like?"

"Rosy-cheeked with a special little twinkle in your eyes." Violet paused, then winked. "Though, I can only imagine having such a handsome man in your bed could do that."

"Violet," Evie said seriously. "I am not going to share intimate details with you."

"What a shame. You are no fun at all," Violet said, with a full pout. She slid herself onto the bench in the water and leaned her head back against the side of the stone around the hot tub. "I take it you haven't been with him long, considering I've never heard about him."

"Yeah, it's...*new,*" was all Evie was prepared to tell Violet. She swirled her arms beneath the water, her skin flushing hotly.

Violet stretched her arms across the stone. "What does your mother think of him? Your father?"

"What do you think of him?" Evie asked.

Violet smiled. "He's special, that one."

"Well, I think anyone who meets Grey thinks that," was all she could say, not wanting to lie to Violet.

Violet's eyes narrowed a little, and then she laughed softly. "Your parents haven't met him, have they?"

Violet always could sniff out an untruth, which was exactly why Evie wouldn't lie to her. Sure, she didn't doubt Violet would understand why she'd brought Grey here. But embarrassment had sunk its claws into Evie, only reminding her how messed up this situation really was. "Well, no, they haven't met yet."

"Why?"

Evie shrugged, the water rippling around her. "We're not that serious."

"Not *that* serious," Violet said, eyes wide. "Oh, please, dear, that man is madly in love with you, so explain to me how you can't be serious. I see the way he watches you. The way he pays attention to all you do. When you move, he reacts. When you smile, his eyes brighten. That's love, my darling. It's not something anyone can hide."

"You always were such a romantic," Evie said, stepping a little farther under the water, her body heat rising.

"Perhaps, but love…" Violet moved to the waterfall, placing her left shoulder underneath, "…real love…that doesn't come around all the time. Lust? Yes, that's something you can find time and time again. But true passion and real love, that's a one-time deal."

Evie imagined Violet believed that. She wasn't sure what she believed. Love was hard, that she knew. "And you think this true passion and real love is something I have with Grey?"

"I know with total certainty that's what you have with him," Violet said firmly. "I see it there on both of your faces. You've found your person, Evie. Don't let him go."

To escape it all for a second, Evie dunked under the water. Here, it was quiet, silent, the jets hammering the water. Everything was peaceful here, perfectly still. Together, their relationship, it was all a lie. Hell, this from the beginning was all a game between them. This weekend was an opportunity to win, she knew that.

Whatever Violet thought she saw, she didn't. Grey played to win, not to love.

Evie broke the water and inhaled the breath her lungs screamed for. "Us…Violet, it's complicated."

"Love always is." Violet turned around, placing the other shoulder under the waterfall. "You both have pasts and scars from your experiences, and right now, you're working out the kinks to set up what you'll be for the rest of your life. If it's complicated, it means you're doing it right. You're getting rid of all the bad stuff that could cloud your happiness. It's a complication that, in the end, will be worth it."

"Is that what you had with Graham?"

Violet's eyes filled with an equal amount of warmth and sadness. "When Graham found me, I'd been broken. I didn't trust anyone. I was defensive. But he was patient and loving. He always said he knew I was meant for him, and he was simply there...never letting me down... never walking away, until eventually, I believed him."

God, their forty-year marriage had been what stories are written about, and his death five years ago had been utterly tragic. "And that's what made Graham the one for you?"

Tears filled Violet's eyes, her voice grew thick. "My dear, that's what made him capture my heart. My life was what it was because he was in it."

Evie's heart bled for Violet, a woman that Evie cared for deeply. Some people would always disappoint because they were blind, either by their own pain or their insecurities. Violet was clear about herself, how she wanted to treat people, and she never wavered. "You must miss him terribly."

Violet sighed. "I survive only because he would want me to. That's my legacy to the man that gave me happiness and peace I wouldn't have known without him, and that, my dear, is what you deserve too. Do not take anything less real or true."

Evie smiled and then took Violet into a soft hug. "I've really missed you."

When Violet leaned away, she smiled. "Maybe this trip is a reminder that you need to come and see me more."

"I think you're right," Evie agreed.

It'd been so long since she was home with friends, people who truly knew her. Sure, her family came up at Christmas to spend a few days with her in Seattle, but she hadn't gone home because she didn't want to see Seth and Holly together. She realized Violet was right—her pain led her life, her wounds weren't scars, they were still bleeding. Her mom knew why. Even her dad understood. But *this*—a talk with someone who saw the world clearly and who knew you inside and out—Evie had forgotten how good this felt.

Maybe in holding on to her heartbreak, she'd forgotten herself.

Chapter 9

Later that day and into the early evening, Grey broke through the water in the small cove on the edge of the Caribbean Sea that was as private as it was gorgeous. An inlet that was owned by the resort and was only accessible to those staying in the presidential suite for a private snorkeling experience. On either side of the small cove were a few caves, and a small beach, but the boat was anchored in the center, the bow facing out toward the North Atlantic Ocean.

Grey glided through the cool water toward the ladder of the speed boat, and tossed his mask, flippers, and snorkel onto the boat's deck and then climbed the ladder. A quick look over his shoulder told him that Evie was still engrossed in the coral reef, her snorkel sticking out of the water. He smiled, never thinking himself someone who cared much for marine life, but Evie's excitement over the fish made the experience a bigger deal.

His earlier conversation with Seth remained on his mind. On the one hand, he thought he should tell Evie about their conversation. On the other hand, he didn't want to ruin this weekend for everyone.

Who knew if Seth now regretted what he said. Perhaps he'd calmed down and realized he made a mistake. That he wanted to marry Holly tomorrow. Grey had no intention of crashing a wedding and hurting Evie. Fuck yeah, he'd protect her against Seth if he dared upset her. But Grey knew he had to let this play out. He couldn't act without seeing what Seth's next move would be.

He took in the state of the boat; the mess from their picnic earlier was still off to the side. Something he didn't intend to worry about until later. He grabbed the towel off the navy pinstriped cushion, trying to recall a time he'd enjoyed an afternoon like he had today. He failed to find anything that could measure up to these last few hours alone with her.

"Amazing."

Evie's sweet voice warmed him, and he glanced over his shoulder, finding her climbing up the ladder. She placed her snorkeling gear next to his and then straightened up. The vision before him made the world disappear and his gaze narrow on her. As it had for the month he'd worked alongside her, hot desire flooded him, making him hot and hard, wanting to get even closer to her.

"Don't move."

Dressed in a black bikini, she froze. Perhaps at the heat in his voice, at the dominance flooding him. Their time together was counting down, and he wouldn't waste any of the minutes he had left. He moved to her, never taking his eyes off her, consumed by the lust raging in her eyes. She'd given him this look many times before now. A look so hot and needy he'd jerked his cock many times thinking of her this way. Before, he couldn't do anything about it, always having to stay professional. Not anymore. Now, he could fully unleash himself, not having to worry about scaring her off, being too much man for her.

When he reached her, he scanned her face, loving the delicate pink-ish hue to her cheeks and the way her lips parted, her breaths seeming harder to drag in. His cock twitched in his swim trunks, throbbing to be deep inside her.

"Be still," he murmured, tangling his fingers into her wet hair, an-gling her head where he wanted it. He dropped his mouth against her neck and kissed from her shoulder to her ear, swirling his tongue, en-joying the way she wiggled her stomach eagerly against his dick. Her sweet, salty taste made him groan. He slid his hand over her bottom, squeezing the fleshy skin. She began moaning, softening beneath his touch, offering herself to him in all the ways he wanted her.

Playing on her enjoyment of voyeurism, he tucked his fingers into the rim of her bathing suit bottoms and slowly pushed them down until she stepped out of them. While he doubted anyone would come by since the resort kept this cove private for its high-paying clients, he almost wished someone would. Even if Evie would likely be em-barrassed, he didn't doubt she'd also find being caught thrilling and exciting.

His cock throbbed as he pulled on the two bows of her bikini top until he had the fabric in his hands. He slid his fingers down her col-larbone, and he stepped in behind her. She gave off a nice little shiver when he bound her wrists together at her back with her bikini top, nice and tight. He liked the way she looked like this, trapped to his desires.

Leaving her standing there with the sun glistening off her tanned skin, he moved to the bench and sat down. He dropped one of the seat cushions onto the floor and hooked a finger at her. "Come here, angel."

"Right away, sir," she joked.

He wasn't joking, and when she moved to him and then dropped to her knees on the cushion, he reached for her, placing her over his thigh.

"Oh, my God." She laughed.

"My way is better, if you recall," he told her gently, rubbing his hand over the roundness of her bottom.

She visibly relaxed over his knee, her head hanging down, her long hair blanketing the deck. He dragged his fingernails up her back and then brought them back down before circling his hand over her bottom again. He waited, moving slowly until she went completely lax, then his hand landed with a heavy thud on her cheek. Her gasp of equal shock and excitement drifted over him.

The sun was hot, beating down on him when he circled his hand again, waiting for her to relax. When she did, he swatted once more. She moaned, unknowingly spreading her legs. He didn't miss the opportunity, giving her exactly what she wanted from him. And he wasn't at all surprised when he slipped his hand between her spread thighs, finding her hot, wet, and ready.

From behind, he swirled her clit, tickling his finger across the bundle of nerves until she wiggled. He knew her body better now, and he fondled her clit until she was gasping. Only then did he place an arm over her back, pinning her to him, then he put all his focus on that sweet ass that had haunted him for a month.

"This is for me, Evie," he murmured. "This is your punishment for all the times you bent over in front of me. Did you do that to tease me?" His hand came down on her ass with a hard slap.

"Yes." She gasped.

"Did it make you wet to know I was watching you…wanting you?"

Another slap on the cheek began to redden her skin.

She moaned and wiggled. "God, yes."

He swatted again, and again, sending her moaning, begging for him. And he didn't stop, not for a second, warming up her lovely skin. Sometimes, he swatted her warm bottom, other times he stroked her slit until she soaked his fingers, beyond ready to take him.

"Did you tease me because you wanted me to fuck you?" he asked, squeezing one bright red cheek then repeating the move on the other.

"Yes, I don't know, maybe," she breathed. "I wanted you to want me. To crave me."

"Is that so?" He assisted her off his lap to kneel on the cushion before him. Keeping his eyes on the lust in the depth of her gaze, he lifted his hips, removing his swim trunks, exposing his hefty cock to her.

She stared at him, nibbling on her lip, and that damn sexy mouth of hers enticed him. He cupped her face, sealing his mouth across hers. She smelled of coconut and sun, as he sucked on her tongue, on her lips, devouring her mouth, informing her that she belonged to him right now.

When he finally broke the kiss and leaned away, he grabbed the base of his cock. "Prepare me to fuck you, angel."

His cock throbbed as he watched her slowly lean forward. With her hands bound behind her, her mouth slid across the tip of his dick. "Fuck," he exhaled, tossing his head back against the edge of the boat.

This, her beautiful mouth, those gorgeous eyes…he needed to see her. He forced his head up to gaze upon her pleasuring him, a bound beauty, moving her head up and down, with the sunscreen on her flesh shining in the sun. "Look at me."

Her heated eyes snapped to his. She bobbed her mouth on the tip, and all his control fled just that easily. She did this to him. There was something there in her eyes, something vulnerable but utterly powerful, and something that drove him crazy.

"Goddamn it," he growled, rising to his feet, grabbing a condom from his wallet resting on the table next to them and applying it quickly. "You're so fucking sexy, Evie. Come here, angel." He reached for her, assisting her onto the bench seat. Her chest rested sideways against the cushion, her reddened bottom available to him. Unable to wait, fueled by this raw desire for her, he kicked her legs open and entered her soaking slit right to the hilt.

She gasped, a heady sound of pleasure. That single noise brought out something primal in him. With fierceness spurring him on, he reached for the wet strands of her hair, fisting it in his hand. "You drive me fucking crazy," he told her, pressing the other hand against her shoulder blades. "Your pussy is so fucking good." He slammed forward, withdrawing quickly to return just as fast.

"Yes!" she screamed, the side of her face pressed against the bench seat, her eyes pinched shut. "You're so hard…God, yes!"

He growled, an inhuman sound, unleashing himself in the way he'd wanted to since he met her. He pounded her sweet pussy until she began to tighten, telling him her climax was rising. Yet so was his.

Wanting to draw this out, he pulled on her arms, bringing her back to his chest, and he switched their positions. He sat on the bench with her on top, the long strands of her hair before him. She didn't miss a step. She moaned loudly now and trembled atop him, expertly riding him to sweet satisfaction. Her reddened ass jiggled perfectly, her moans mixed alongside his. He gripped her bound wrists with one hand, and then held onto her hip, assisting her, sweat dripping down the side of his face. She rode his cock and began panting, her tight pussy a vise grip, telling him yet again she was right there and ready to dive into the pleasure.

He wasn't ready for this to end. Not yet. He reached forward with his free hand and massaged one breast and then the other, tweaking her nipples tightly. She moaned against the bite and moved harder now… faster. Anything less than exploding against him wasn't acceptable today.

He didn't only want to be a weekend memory for her.

He wanted to be her greatest fuck of all time.

Determined, and with another low growl, he was on his feet again, one arm across her chest, the other around her waist, supporting her. He didn't pause and let her high fade, he pounded into her from behind. Skin against skin, every one of his thrusts grew more intense as the seconds drew on until he set a rhythm that didn't give her a chance to refuse his call. His cock was straining to blow, hitting the perfect spot inside her, and the loss of control he heard in her screams tightened his balls.

Sweat glistened along his body with each hard and unforgiving shift of his hips. His muscles strained and burned. Needing her to come with him, he assisted her forward, helping her rest against the edge of the boat, and rocked his hips harder.

With his other hand, he grabbed her hair none too gently, tipping her head back. In her ear, he growled, "You want to come, Evie?"

"Yes," she screamed, her soaked pussy quivering against him.

Owned by him, he moved harder, faster, pushing his muscles to their very limit. "Make me come with you."

And with her ravenous screams and pussy pulsating against him, she did. With force, making him near cross-eyed, his semen exploded into the condom, and he bucked and jerked his pleasure.

As his strength left him, so did hers, and she sank down all the way to the deck. On her side, she looked up at him and laughed, a sound of pure happiness and satisfaction. He couldn't smile with her. Something potent and raw washed through him, tightening his throat and chest.

He squatted down before her, taking her chin in his grip, and she suddenly went quiet, looking back at him. The exchange between them was long and intense. "Are you going to tease me again with that fine ass of yours?"

She grinned. "When I can move again, that's a big fat yes."

REDRESSED IN HER bikini, Evie stepped back onto the boat's deck, returning from the cabin and bringing the two glasses of white wine she'd gone to fetch. She found Grey back in his swim trunks and sprawled out on the bow's cockpit. His arms were resting behind him, chin tilted up, eyes fixated on the sun beginning to set over the horizon. Sculpted, hard lines, rough masculine beauty, his thick muscular arm covered in shaded tattoos; Grey was what men aimed to be, right down to his spectacular cock.

Though, as she approached him, she wondered if she truly knew him, the *real* Greyson Crawford, the man behind the sexy smile and extravagant lifestyle, beyond his sinful touches? They only had this wedding weekend together, could you truly know someone in only three days?

When she approached, he glanced her way, his eyes going from peaceful to heated in an instant. "Stop there for a minute," he murmured.

She froze. "What now?"

"It's just you," he said, cocking his head, giving her a very thorough once-over before reaching her gaze again. "There, under the sunlight like that, you're perfect. Let me remember it."

She melted a little bit and smiled. "All about the romance today?"

"Is it working?" he asked with a grin.

"Most definitely." She laughed and began walking toward him again, and offered him one of the glasses.

He winked, accepting the glass. "Then I'll lay it on thick."

She chuckled softly and sat next to him on the blanket that he had laid out. With a long exhale, she glanced out at the quiet, mid-deep, aqua-colored water, and sipped the expensive wine with the citrus hints. "We only have another hour or so before we have to head back."

Grey took a big sip of the wine and frowned. "I don't approve of this sleepover Holly has planned."

"Of course you don't because that means no sex for you tonight." At his deeper frown, she laughed softly. "Sadly, it's part of my maid of honor duties, and honestly, I haven't spent much time with her, so you're going to have to suck it up."

Alpha male irritation sprinkled the air, but Grey nodded. "I'll have to make do without you then."

Evie hesitated, wondering what he'd do without her. Then she reminded herself that he had just fucked the living shit out of her and he was hers for the weekend. She smiled. "Poor, baby."

He smiled behind his wine glass. "Poor me, indeed."

She shook her head at him, staring off into the distance at the white caps, and sipped her wine. But her mind circled back to the guy beside her. "So," she said, turning back to him, "is it my turn for a little Q and A?"

Grey lowered his wine glass to the deck, giving her his full attention. "Sure, why not."

She pondered all the things she wanted to know about Grey, who kept surprising her, including bringing her to this cove today. Though considering what they'd just done, there was one thought that stood out from the rest… "Do you like normal sex?"

His eyebrow winged up. "What is *normal* sex?"

"I mean, like touching sex." She glanced at the water, hating how her cheeks flushed. "Intimate sex."

"Because I bind you, you mean?"

She looked his way and nodded. "Exactly."

After examining her for a few long seconds, he added, "No, it's not the sex I usually have."

"Why is that?" She wasn't sure why she needed to know, but she did.

His brows furrowed when he looked at the water. The boat rocked a little, and then he turned to her again and explained, "Because it complicates things for women."

"You mean that the intimacy makes things too emotional?"

"For them, yes," he agreed, inclining his head. "I used to allow sex without the kink, but I noticed that if a woman could touch my face during sex, let's just say…it became too personal."

Evie pondered that, and after thinking about it, she concluded, "Are you sure that it didn't become too personal for you and that's what you had a problem with?"

He glanced away, and the firm set of his mouth told her he didn't intend on answering her.

It didn't matter, she didn't need him to. "It's a boundary you place. I get that. And I guess I respect that, too. You don't want to hurt anyone." His soft eyes came to hers, something passing between them in that moment, and she smiled. "Actually, it's kind of sweet that you do that because you think you're protecting your lovers."

He reached for her hand and kissed her palm.

How confusing was he? For a guy who clearly hated intimacy, he was pretty damn good at it. Leaving that behind for now, not wanting him to shut down, she changed the subject. "All right then, tell me this: why do you play this cold-hearted, skirt-chasing ladies' man?"

He snorted and heaved a long heavy sigh. "I'm beginning to regret saying yes to having this conversation." She laughed, and he added, "But do explain, what do you mean by *play* it?"

"You're not that guy," she explained, crossing her legs and resting her wine glass between them. "I see that now, but when I first met you…it's like you've got this wall up, keeping everyone out. I've seen you turn it on in front of strangers like it's second nature. So, what is it, a nasty ex-girlfriend who broke your heart, a lover that moved away? What's got your heart all tangled up in knots, Greyson Crawford?" She took a sip of her wine.

"It's actually none of those things," he said, the sunlight shimmering on his cheekbone. "I had girlfriends in the past. A couple of them throughout high school, but that was young affection." He drank back another big sip of his wine and added, "In college, I partied a lot."

"With your friend, Maddox?"

"That's right," he said, dipping his chin. "Our lifestyle at that time never led to a girlfriend. It's not that I didn't want one, but I was a young kid, and I liked…" He paused and then smirked. "I liked women—and a lot of them." Another pause. Then, "I've witnessed many relationships end in pain. If I were to put myself through that, I'd want it to be right, something like I've seen from my parents or even what Maddox has now with his wife, Joss. But I've never had that personally before, so I never wanted to be tied down."

"No, you wanted to tie them up."

He barked a laugh. "Truer words have never been spoken."

Evie hesitated and drew in a deep breath, pondering his relationship history. Her life had simply been so different. She'd been madly in love up until college. But Grey was right, it was young affection. She knew that her *forever* relationship would look a lot different than what she had with Seth.

In the silence, Grey's eyebrow arched. "Does hearing about my past upset you?"

"No," she replied, softly shaking her head. "I actually appreciate your honesty. It's refreshing."

"It's refreshing to you because you've been hurt before," Grey said, giving her a measured look. "That'll leave a mark."

She stopped with her wine halfway to her lips and frowned at him. "Are you saying that I'm damaged goods?"

He grasped her chin, tilting her eyes to meet the amusement in his. "What I'm saying is that there's a mark on your soul because of what Seth and Holly did to you. Marks like that either make you stronger or weaken you."

"What's my mark? The latter or the former?"

"You know the answer to that question, not me." He lowered his hand, glanced out at the water again, resting his arms on his knees. "But no matter what, we can't be strong all the time. Sometimes, you need to break fully in order to heal."

Evie took a sip of wine, and while citrusy hints lingered on her tongue, she realized now that the mark Grey mentioned had weakened her for years. She had reacted defensively for a long time. And if she were honest with herself, she could feel, even now, that sore spot on her soul that told her why she hadn't had a solid relationship since Seth. It wasn't that she still loved him, it was that she no longer trusted anyone.

That's what she liked the most about Grey, she realized. His world was solid. That meant something. "So, back to you," she said. "You've never broken a heart or two?"

"Upset, probably," he said, "But have I left a woman heartbroken? No, it's not my way. I'm clear with what I want, and I don't get involved with women who I don't think can handle the arrangements we set."

"Like ours?"

He gave a knowing smile, tipping his wine glass at her. "With you, there was a little more on the line because you're not the type of woman to have a one-night stand with a guy like me."

"Which brings us back to my original point," she said. "You're not a ladies' man with me. That part hasn't come out when we've been together. Not since you first suggested joining me this weekend. It's why I agreed to the arrangement. You're different."

His brow winged up again. "Do I truly act differently, or are you perhaps seeing me in a different way because you're finally letting me in?"

She paused and sipped her wine, stumped.

Could that be true?

Was he softening, or was she simply opening up to him? "It's both," she decided after a minute of thinking it over. "You're definitely not the cutthroat, stern, far too arrogant businessman I've known these past weeks. You're not the overly charming ladies' man either. But, yes, maybe I see life differently than before." The moment her mouth shut, she realized he'd distracted her again from digging a bit deeper into his life. "And will you stop trying to change the subject?"

He chuckled, shaking his head. "Honestly, Evie, there's not much to know here. It wasn't that I never planned to date long-term or find that special someone. When I finished college, I hit the ground running to make my company successful. There wasn't time for a steady relationship, and if I did have a girlfriend, they always broke it off because I picked work over them."

"You never once chose them?"

He finished off his wine. "No. Never," he finally answered.

"You don't think that's kinda cold?" she asked, quickly looking at the birds soaring overhead.

"I think it's very cold," he agreed, "but business is a cold thing. I didn't have time to worry if I was hurting a woman's feelings. So, I was always clear. If they wanted sex, I could give them that. Hell, I could even date and take them out sometimes. But if business came up, they came second. That was the deal they had to accept."

She sipped her still half-full glass of wine to pause the conversation, giving her time to think. It was hard to see Grey the way he described. He simply didn't seem like the cold guy who only cared about his job. He had more passion in his pinky finger than Seth had in his whole body. But could he turn it off so easily? "I'm beginning to see why some women in your past had a problem with that."

He nodded. "I never said it was fair, only that it happened."

The boat rocked against a small wave, and she watched her wine swish in her glass before she addressed him again. "Do you regret how you treated women in your past?"

"Regret?" He paused, brows drawn, then shook his head. "No, I don't regret anything I've done. I did it for a reason, and I trust my instincts. But I also never hurt anyone like you've been hurt because we never got that close. It simply never happened. At the end of the day, my business was my *priority*."

"And now?"

"Now, my business is solid."

There were a lot of things unsaid between them, and all the unspoken words felt heavy in the air.

Obviously, he felt it too since he broke the silence. "You, angel," he said, reaching for her, "are looking far too serious." He wrapped an arm around her back, guiding her to straddle him. "Now come here and kiss me before we start dissecting my past and breaking it into all my painful memories."

"Were there painful memories?"

He chuckled and flipped their positions until she was lying on her back against the deck and he was resting between her thighs. Hovering over her, he frowned. "Evie, what did we agree upon?"

"Your game. Your rules. My surrender."

"Precisely," he said firmly. "Now, kiss me."

This time, she listened.

Chapter 10

With the sun now nearly set, Grey held Evie's hand, passing door after door until they reached room 1089. He wanted her with him tonight, and he didn't particularly enjoy handing Evie off to Holly, even if he understood the reasons behind it. Today had been a good day...a great day, even, and he wasn't thrilled that the night was ending without Evie being naked and beneath him.

When they reached the door, before she could knock, he tugged her against him, nice and close. She angled her head back and wrapped her arms around his waist, smiled. "Thank you for earlier," he told her, brushing his knuckles across her cheek where the light from the sconce on the wall cast a soft glow across her skin.

"Thank *you* for earlier," she said with a laugh, leaning into his touch. "It wasn't a bad way to spend an afternoon."

He arched an eyebrow at her. "Not a bad way?"

"Yeah," she said slowly, then after a couple strode by with their young son, she winked. "You know, because men always hand deliver paradise and orgasms to me."

"So spoiled you are." He chuckled, sliding her hair off her shoulder and cupping her nape.

"Totally spoiled," she retorted, grabbing the back of his tank top. Something changed in her expression then, becoming a little sweeter, maybe even more honest. "I can't really thank you enough for today. It was pretty spectacular."

"It was certainly that." He dragged his thumb up her neck, watching the way heat rose in her eyes. Her reactions to him were unlike anything he'd seen before from any woman. He had yet to figure out if it was *him* or if she simply held this level of passion naturally. Whatever it was, he found her heated reactions addictive, tempting him to stay in Punta Cana longer, simply to hold onto it.

Unable to help himself, he licked his lips and brought his mouth to hers. Before, whenever he'd kissed Evie in front of others, it was to prove a point, to show them that what he and she had was real. Maybe to even prove to Evie what he could do to her. Now, he took her in his arms and sealed his mouth across hers only for himself. His kiss was sweet but possessive, and she melted into every second of it.

"Oh, good, you're here," said Holly, whisking her door wide open. "Did you knock? I didn't hear you."

"Not yet, no," Evie rasped, her heated eyes on Grey. Then she blinked and smiled at Holly. "Are you ready for some girl time?"

Holly smiled. "Don't you know it."

The moment broken, Grey released Evie and stepped back, fighting against the heat pinging between them. "Until tomorrow," he said.

She moved inside the room, holding the door. "Until tomorrow."

Her sweet smile was the last thing he saw before he was staring at the closed door. His chest was tight, shoulders tense. Christ, was it the romantic atmosphere, the lack of stress, or was it simply *her* that made him…anticipate missing her?

Silently pondering this new development, he moved toward the open doorway that led back to the pathway toward the beach. Exercise always centered him, and the ocean shouted to him for an evening swim before calling it a night.

Just as he neared the beach, an unusual ringtone on his cell phone had him reaching into the pocket of his swim trunks. Immediately, he understood why the ringtone sounded so different. He'd never Face-timed anyone on his cell phone before, only on his computer. "Hello, Mother," he said, answering the phone and taking a seat on the bench facing the beach.

"Where are you?" his mother asked. Short, shiny, silver hair, a soft coat of makeup against skin that appeared younger than her sixty-five years due to some well-placed Botox, Anne Crawford looked like a movie star more than one of Seattle's socialites. She squinted her bright blue eyes, clearly trying to examine the view behind him.

"I'm in Punta Cana," Grey answered, stretching his arm out across the back of the bench.

"Punta Cana, how strange," Anne said, eyes wide with surprise. From the big bay window behind her, she was clearly sitting in her favorite rocking chair out on the porch of her mansion overlooking Lake Washington. "Why are you there?"

"Yes, Grey," a low voice said. "Please do explain."

Grey chuckled, recognizing the voice. "Hello, Maddox."

The phone angled, the screen blurring for a moment before Maddox's angular face filled the screen. His appearance was not a surprise.

Maddox spent more time with Anne than Grey did. Grey appreciated that, too. Anne had loosened her tight grip a smidgen once Maddox came into the picture.

"Hello, Grey." Maddox smiled, crinkling the corners of his blue eyes, a strand of gelled light-brown hair falling out of place.

At the gleam in his closest friend's eyes, he got right to the point. "Now, before either of you start drilling me, I came here to attend a wedding with a friend—Evie."

Maddox gave a shit-eating grin. "Oh, Anne, he's with a woman. This sounds serious."

"Give me back that phone."

More rustling, then Anne's frown appeared on the screen. "Who is this Evie and why have I not heard about her before? Are you serious? How long have you been dating? Why haven't you brought her to see me?"

Maddox laughed.

Grey sighed. "Mother, take a breath."

Anne simply stared back at him. "You haven't answered me, Greyson."

Another sigh as Grey hesitated while a couple strode by him on the beach. Then, "Evie is an interior designer who lives in Seattle," he explained, keeping to the facts and hoping that'd be enough for his mother. "No, we're not serious, it's a new thing. That's why I haven't brought her out to see you."

"But you had no problem taking her to the Dominican Republic?"

"Well, that's complicated."

Maddox interjected, "Complicated doesn't sound like your speed, buddy."

Grey heaved another long sigh. "We're here for the weekend. This isn't a big deal."

Anne took a few long seconds to clearly absorb the information and then her eyes narrowed. "You're lying to me, but we can talk more about this when you get home. Maddox and I need more sweet tea."

The screen somersaulted again before Maddox's face appeared. "I have to agree with Anne. This Evie"—he gave a sly smile—"she's got you ruffled."

"I am not...*ruffled*." Grey snorted.

"I call bullshit." Maddox grinned, pointing at the screen. "You like this one. Dare I ask...is that a twinkle in your eye?"

"I can see it, too," his mother called from a distance.

Grey shook his head and glanced out at the beach, taking in the ocean for miles around. What he'd give to be in that water and not being grilled. "All right," he said, glancing back at Maddox, ready for this to be over with. "You got your revenge." Which was his due, considering Grey had put Maddox in a similar hot seat with Anne when he met his now wife, Joss. "You can stop encouraging her anytime."

Maddox chuckled and nodded, then waited, glancing to his left, then back to Grey again. "She's gone inside now." He leaned in closer to the screen, brows furrowed, concentrating on Grey intently. "We don't have long, so be quick. Why are you there with the woman you told me was hands-off?"

He'd mentioned Evie to Maddox, more than a few times. "Well," he said, choosing his words carefully, keeping in mind that his mother might overhear what he said. "Her contract with my company ended, which made the dynamics of our relationship change. She needed an escort for the wedding of her best friend and Evie's ex-boyfriend, and

I'm her date."

Maddox frowned. "Whoa. You're right. This is complicated. Sounds like there's a story there."

"There is," Grey agreed, crossing one ankle over his knee, watching a mother chase after her child running away from her on the beach. "Regardless, it's been quite the trip."

Maddox's stern eyes searched Grey's before he added, "Is a date all that you are to her?"

"I've enjoyed her, if that's what you're getting at." It was all Grey was prepared to say on the matter. "But this woman…she's…*good*."

Maddox began to grin. Before he could say anything more, Grey's mother's voice suddenly sounded off in the distance, telling him that she'd come back outside. "When are you coming back?" she asked.

"Monday afternoon," Grey replied, not minding the interruption. That smile of Maddox's had been sly enough that Grey knew Maddox's next comment would likely only annoy him. "After the wedding—"

"The wedding?" His mother's face suddenly filled the screen; obviously, she'd stolen the phone from Maddox. "Greyson Crawford, you'd better not be getting married without me there."

"Mother." He sighed.

"Don't let him off the hook," Maddox called out, clearly wanting to stir up shit in the way Grey had stirred things up for Maddox before. "Seems to me he's hiding things. I bet he *is* getting married."

"Are you?" Anne asked sternly. "Oh, you'd better not be. I will be so angry at you."

Again, Grey sighed. "Mother, I love you, and I would never get married without you there. I'll see you in a couple of days."

"Greyson—"

"Goodbye." He ended the call and smiled down at his phone. His mother was fiercely protective and intrusive, a total helicopter parent. He loved her, but he also didn't tolerate it. Somehow, over the years, she'd accepted it.

He drew in a long, deep breath and looked out at the water, staring at the bright moon and twinkling stars. As a pelican flew out over the water before dipping down and scooping up its dinner, he realized every woman in his past had been more trouble than not, except for one.

Evie.

———

THE DOOR CLICKED shut, and Evie smiled, closing her eyes as a flurry of emotions pinned her to the spot. How unexpected all this was. Originally, she'd thought coming to the wedding would be emotionally taxing. Yet, somehow, she'd flourished here in ways she never dreamed of. Life was so full of funny surprises—good surprises.

"Thanks for coming to stay with me tonight," Holly said from behind Evie.

She snapped herself out of her personal euphoria, reminded that this time was for Holly, and she turned around. "Don't be silly. I wanted to stay with you." She kicked off her flip-flops, as Holly jumped onto the king-size bed in the bridal suite.

Evie moved farther into the room. She'd never thought of herself as a materialistic person before, not caring about those things much. But she couldn't help but notice that the room Grey had gotten for them made this room look small in comparison. That realization, matched with her entire weekend with Grey, and she thought: *finally, my grass is greener.*

She'd never once pitied herself when it came to Seth breaking her heart all those years ago. She kept her head down and worked hard. But her heart reminded her now that it was nice when someone spoiled her. That someone appreciated her enough to put her first. Maybe she even forgot how that once felt.

When Evie neared the bed, spotting the wedding dress still in the bag hanging above the balcony doors, Holly added, "I imagine being away from Grey must suck."

"It's okay, really," Evie said, stopping near the mini bar beneath the television set. "Grey rented a boat and we spent some time together on the water. He got lots of me, and I've barely had any time with you." Which was the truth.

The old Evie would have given Holly all her time. With Grey here, he hadn't allowed that to happen, and she rather enjoyed that. She liked this new version of herself. She didn't feel like she was giving too much to anyone. More so, she was giving more to herself. "Want a drink?" she asked Holly.

"Oh, yeah," Holy said, bouncing on the bed. "I had the hotel staff bring us up a big bottle of wine for tonight."

"Goodie." Evie smiled, grabbing the wine bottle from the fridge. "Are you excited for the wedding tomorrow?"

"I'm somewhere between excited and nervous," Holly explained when Evie uncorked the wine and began pouring the sparkling white into the two tall glasses.

"Totally understandable, I'm sure." Evie recorked the wine, returned the bottle to the fridge, and moved to the bed, offering Holly the glass. "But it's going to be a great day." She sat cross-legged across from Holly, just as she'd done so many times while growing up. "Remember when we used to do this back in high school, stay up all night long and talk?"

Holly smiled. "It feels like no time has passed at all."

"I know, it's crazy." Evie smiled, realizing, in all this, she was glad she'd come. For Seth. For Holly. They all had history together, and this was a very important time in their lives. With warmth filling her soul, she, for the first time ever, was genuinely happy for them. Maybe it was Grey, maybe it was the orgasmic glow. Or maybe she needed this closure too, because suddenly, a weight was lifted that she hadn't realized was there before.

"Everything has changed, hasn't it?" Holly suddenly said, voice soft and low.

"What do you mean?" Evie asked, resting her wine glass on her thigh.

"I mean, remember how it used to be?" Holly's gaze cast downward at her fingers fiddling with the strings on her worn jean shorts. "How we did everything together, totally inseparable." She glanced up, tears in her eyes. "Remember those times?"

"Yeah, I do," Evie said and smiled. "They're happy memories for me."

"I miss those times," Holly whispered, wiping at a fallen tear. "How simple and fun they were. Do you ever miss how things used to be in high school?"

"Sometimes," Evie admitted with a little shrug. "Things were definitely easier. Well, maybe still emotionally terrible and confusing, but easier."

Holly nodded, staring down into her wine glass before addressing

Evie again. "I miss who I was back then." She paused. Then, "I guess I miss us."

Evie drew in a long, deep breath, figuring Holly was getting whatever closure she needed as well to embark on this new stage of her life tomorrow. Knowing that, and feeling better about things than she'd ever felt before, she said, "It's so strange where life takes you. Back in high school, I never would have believed that I'd move to Seattle and have a business that's all mine."

"You've changed so much in such a good way," Holly said with a soft smile. "You've evolved into this amazing woman."

"I have found my happy nook."

Holly's brows rose. "What's a happy nook?"

Evie took a quick sip of her wine then set to explaining, "It's my own little piece of the world that belongs only to me. My business. My life. My happiness." She'd chased her dreams along the way, and she caught them.

"I wish I had done that." Holly chugged back a good portion of her wine.

Evie sipped her Moscato, pausing a moment, reassessing Holly's mood. "You've evolved into an amazing woman, too."

"No, I haven't." Holly gave a measured look, her shoulders slumped. "I'm the exact same person you knew in high school. The only difference is that I'm now older and work as a paralegal. I live on the same street as my parents. I do the same thing every single day."

"Oh, stop it. You have an amazing life," Evie countered, placing a hand on Holly's leg, giving it a squeeze. "A good life with Seth."

"I do have a good life with him, you're right." Holly nodded, drawing in a long breath before continuing. "But it's the life I knew I'd have.

You have so much excitement in yours, and I'm so jealous of that. You have this amazing guy who makes you shine in ways I've never seen anyone light up. You're so different than the Evie I used to know."

"Is that a good thing?" Evie wondered.

Holly laughed softly, bouncing the mattress a little, and nodded. "It's a great thing, but it makes me green with envy."

Evie took another sip of her wine, aware of something now she hadn't considered before. She'd thought she wanted Seth and Holly to be jealous of her. Now that Holly clearly was, it seemed wrong, nasty even. And not the Evie she wanted to be. "Every life has its flaws." Hers, of course, being the fact that her relationship with Grey was based on lies. While it'd come to feel more real now, it was also temporary, not what Holly thought it to be. "And my life certainly isn't perfect."

"Looks pretty darn great to me," Holly countered. She took another big, long sip of her wine, and then her expression changed, becoming darker, tears filling her eyes again. "Do you hate me, Evie?"

"No, of course not." She squeezed Holly's leg again, trying to comfort. "Why would you even say that?"

Holly hung her head. "Because of what I did to you? Because I took Seth."

Evie's chest tightened, but she forced the words out, knowing she needed to say it aloud for herself, and Holly clearly needed to hear it. "You didn't take Seth from me. I left to go to college, remember?" Holly looked up then, big tears in her eyes, and Evie added, "I left you both. You looked to each other, and you fell in love."

A tear spilled down her cheek, chin trembling. "How can you not hate me for that?"

"Because I don't. You're my longest, closest friend. You know me like no one does, and I know you would have never been with him unless you madly loved him." She hesitated, then she realized in all this there was a point that stood out above all else. "You two are really happy together, so I *am* happy for both of you that you found your forever in each other."

Holly's face slowly began to brighten. Evie realized they'd never done this. Talked it out, and Evie knew why. It'd been too hard before. Maybe she had truly gotten past all this. Life had such a weird way of working things out. All she'd needed was Grey to see that the past was the past for a very good reason.

"I'm happy for you, too," Holly said, wiping away her tears from her pink cheeks. "Grey's amazing and charming and simply sexy as hell."

"Oh, yeah," Evie agreed. "He's all those things and more."

"You deserve that." Holly grabbed Evie's hand, squeezing tightly. "I hope you know that. You deserve all the good things."

"As do you." Evie carefully held her wineglass in her hand and then wrapped her arms around Holly. It wasn't until then that Evie realized Holly needed this hug, maybe more than Evie did. She felt her tension in the tight way Holly hugged her back.

It was funny how life worked out sometimes. As Holly leaned away, and Evie stared at her best friend in the world, so much history between them, it was like she stared into a mirror. The life Holly had now might have been Evie's if she hadn't chased after her dreams. Now, she had her life, and she happened to like it. A lot.

"Okay, no more tears," Holly said with a smile, wiping away the remainder of her tears from her face quickly. "We have tonight. Tomorrow, I'll be a married woman, and you'll be headed back to Seattle." She raised her wine glass. "To happiness. To friendship. To love."

Evie clanged her glass against Holly's, feeling all the broken pieces inside her sealing back together again. "To happiness. To friendship. To love."

The morning of the wedding, sweat poured off Grey's body as he pushed himself harder on his run along the beach, the sun beating down on his bare upper body, his sport shorts clinging to his thighs. Water splashed up, his shoes were soaking wet, but none of that mattered on his run. The hot air, the bright, sunny day—he decided he needed to vacation more often. Christ, maybe it was time to purchase a vacation home in the tropics. He'd been missing out, and it was Evie that reminded him how he hadn't been living, not truly, not like he did in his twenties. He'd been working, pushing hard to make his company successful. Perhaps it was time for a new chapter in his life.

When he reached the bar at the resort, he slowed to a stop, bent over, and breathed deeply, recovering from the run. The world was quiet around him. Being eight in the morning, most vacationers were either having breakfast or likely still fast asleep. Grey lifted his arms, stretching his shoulders, his legs tight and sore as he strode back to his room in the first block of buildings on the left. The wedding wasn't until this afternoon, but Grey wanted to be there for Evie when she returned to the room before leaving to do all the girly things she needed to do today.

Once he reached his door, he heard voices coming from inside. Loud voices. Using his keycard, he opened the door and entered the room. It took him a good few seconds to take in the view in front of him.

Holly sat on the couch nearest him, tears raining down her cheeks, her black makeup streaking her face. Seth stood by the balcony door, hands stuffed into his pockets, his head hanging, his shoulders hunched. Grey glanced left then, finding Evie, and his focus narrowed entirely on her. She stood near the bed, wearing only a house coat, her wet hair still dripping, telling Grey she'd *just* stepped out of the shower. Though it was her pale skin and wide eyes that concerned him the most.

"Are you all right?" he asked, moving to her immediately.

"I don't know what I am," she said slowly, obviously in a state of shock.

Grey looked from Seth to Holly then back to Evie. Immediately, he understood what was happening here. But he wouldn't voice that thought in case he was wrong. Instead, he asked no one in particular, "What's going on here?"

"What's going on here…" Holly said, sobbing, "…is that Seth is still in love with Evie."

"Oh, God," Evie whispered, dropping her head into her hands. "Please stop saying that." She drew in a long, deep breath then lifted her head, eyes on Seth. "You don't love me. You love the old me, and that's okay. But I'm not that young girl anymore. You love Holly. You two are meant to be together. This is simply cold feet. That's all." Her worried gaze came to Grey's, obviously seeking help.

Grey sighed and looked at Seth. "You do realize you are getting married this afternoon."

Hands still in his pockets, he half shrugged. "I had to be honest."

"Honest!" Holly yelled, jumping to her feet, her fists clenched at her sides. "Now you *need* to be honest, on our wedding day? Why weren't you honest before? You could have told me all this. Why are you doing this to me?"

Seth glanced at his feet again. "I know, I know. I'm sorry, Holly."

"Sorry?" she screamed, her face bright red. "You are not fucking sorry. If you were, you never would have done this."

Grey glanced at Evie again, and he took her hand, feeling her tremble. She looked at him then, telling him all he needed to know. She'd been completely blindsided by Seth's admission and had no idea how to handle it. Luckily for her, Grey did. "I'm not sure why you need to discuss this in here," he said sternly, glancing at Holly. "This is between you and Seth. I suggest you take this conversation somewhere more private."

Holly appeared to not even hear Grey and glared daggers at Seth. "I can't believe you're doing this to me. Evie doesn't love you anymore. She doesn't want you. She loves Grey. Can't you see it? It's written all over her face."

Evie dropped her gaze, cheeks flushed.

Grey stroked her hand, letting her know he was there. With her.

"Oh, my God," Holly cried, covering her face with her hands. "My parents, my family…everyone is here, Seth. What will we tell them?"

Seth all but whispered, "We'll get it figured out."

"We'll get it figured out," Holly repeated, slowly lowering her hands, scowling. "I want nothing to do with you." She turned to Evie. "You have to help me, Evie."

Evie suddenly stiffened, and Grey noticed the way her eyes and mouth tightened. Holly had hit a nerve. A big nerve.

Evie drew in a long, deep breath, and when she spoke, her voice was firm but also hinted at sadness. "I never wanted any of this. Don't you both know that?" All eyes came to her, and she glanced from Seth to Holly. "I didn't want you to fall in love and yet, you did, so I made myself accept it."

Grey wrapped his other hand around hers, holding one of hers in both of his, feeling her shaking now as she continued. "I didn't want you to get married, but then you got engaged, and yes, it hurt me at first…" She paused. Then added. "No, hurt isn't strong enough. You broke me."

"Evie," Holly whispered, all the anger in her voice gone, tears in her eyes for another reason altogether.

Evie held up her hands. "Please. Let me finish." She shut her eyes, breathed deeply, and then faced them again. "I accepted your relationship because I care for you. Both of you. And I built a life of my own that I'm proud of. I truly wanted you to be happy."

The pain in Evie's expression tightened Grey's chest, strangling the air right out of him. She hid nothing of what they made her feel, and he saw the ripple of that across Seth's and Holly's faces. Both were crying now, lost in their blame, in their shame.

Evie never wavered, baring her soul in a way that made Grey only able to see her.

"I accepted you two being together because I thought you found true love in each other's arms." Her voice blistered. Something changed in Grey then, he felt it course through him, a subtle change that he couldn't stop, making him soften to Evie, when she added, "Real love. Love that can't be stopped because it's that powerful. Love that would make you hurt your best friend and your ex-girlfriend, not because you wanted to, but because it was something that you couldn't deny."

Grey stepped closer, unable to stop himself, as her expression became so haunted. He slid his hand across her back, and he didn't like that he got no response. He thought maybe she'd cringe, tell him that it was too much, or maybe she'd lean into him for support. But the coldness concerned him.

There was nothing but her pain when she continued. "I believed you two being together was fate. That you were meant to be with each other all this time, and how could I stand in the way of that? I wanted, after all this, for something good to come out of so much pain. I came here to support you." A tear spilled from her eye, and she brushed it away quickly when she added, "Last night, I truly let it all go and felt genuinely happy that you two had found each other. I got closure. I moved on." She drew in a long, deep breath, narrowing accusing eyes on Seth. "But now you tell me it wasn't real. That your feelings for Holly aren't real? Look at her. She's standing here with her heart broken and for what? Because one woman isn't enough. You have to have all the toys for yourself?"

She stepped away from Grey, approached them both and said, "There's so much I could say right now." To Seth, she stated, "Like, do you honestly think you can have whatever you want, hurt whomever you want, that somehow you're entitled to keep changing your mind about the woman you want to be with? Well, let me be the first to finally tell you…you can't." To Holly, her voice softened, "I'm sorry you're hurting. I'm sorry that this is happening to you. It's not what I would have wanted." Her eyes shut, and she drew in another deep breath before facing them again. "In the end, all I want to say is, don't bring me into this mess. There's a lot I can take, but *that* is the one thing I can't. Because I, out of anyone in this entire fucked-up situation, don't deserve it. Do I make myself perfectly clear?"

Heads hanging, both Seth and Holly nodded.

Evie spun on her heels, moved to the door, and yanked it open. "Now, go and talk this out." She pointed to the doorway. "If you're getting married, let me know, and I'll be there. If you're not, then I wish you two nothing but the best going forward." She paused. Then, with exasperation, she stated, "Get out. Be grown-ups and deal with your shit."

Holly rose first and, after hugging Evie, swiftly left the room, a blubbering mess with a pathetic Seth dragging his feet after her.

When Seth passed Grey, he asked, "Did you warn her?"

"No," was Grey's only reply.

The door slammed shut, and Grey regarded Evie as she moved closer, cautiously, but the distance was slowly killing him. He strode forward, reaching her in two big strides, taking her in his arms. "I'm sorry you had to go through that, Evie."

She tensed.

Alarmed, he leaned away, discovering her eyes now narrowed on him.

"Did you know that Seth felt this way?"

It was his turn to heave a long sigh. "Yes, Evie, I knew."

GREY'S WORDS BURNED across Evie, smacking into her like a fist, and she took a step back, trying to understand why exactly this stung so bad. Regardless, for the first time since he entered the room, she actually got a good look at him. Dressed in black sport shorts that stopped at the knee, socks, and runners, he wore nothing else. His hair and skin glistened with the lingering sweat from his obvious workout, the sleeve of tattoos on his arm brighter than usual, his muscles seemingly more defined. Whether that was from the run he'd done before he entered the room, or the tension now between them, she didn't know. But his chest seemed thicker, abs cut to perfection, even that sexy V there a treat for the eyes. Though none of that could distract her from a harsh truth she didn't want to believe. "When did Seth tell you he had doubts about the wedding?" she asked, trying to make sense out of all this.

"When we went golfing."

Evie blinked, absorbing that. "You knew since yesterday?"

"Yes."

"Why didn't you tell me?" she asked, the walls slowly beginning to close in, the ground rocky beneath her bare feet.

"Because it wasn't my truth to tell." His gaze hardened with each word, voice turning back into his business voice. "We had this weekend together. I wanted to enjoy you, not upset you."

Her heart clenched, hurt in ways that felt all too familiar, but somehow it was even rawer now. And how confusing was that? She wasn't supposed to become attached to Grey, that had never been the plan. "Did you tell him that it was up to me if I wanted to be with him?" she asked.

"Of course, I told him that," Grey replied, though there was no softness in his voice, only conviction in the choice *he* made. "It is your choice. Even if you chose him now, I would not stand in your way." His eyes narrowed, mouth pinched tightly before he added, "But I don't give a shit about Seth. Nor would I help him get you back into his life."

She paused and drew in a long, deep breath, thinking everything through. Of course, she understood Grey's point. Still, his reasoning felt cold, detached, so *not* the relationship she'd ever see herself in. "You didn't say anything else to him?" she asked.

"Why would I?" He took a step forward as if that settled everything.

"No." She raised her hand, stopping him. "Please don't." Her mind swam with questions. He sounded so reasonable, but there was a thought tickling the back of her mind that she couldn't reach.

"Evie, come here." He held his arms wide. "Don't be mad."

"No," she finally said, swallowing down humiliation. "You're right. I shouldn't be mad at you about any of this. We had a deal, and your deal didn't include looking out for me. I'm sorry. I shouldn't have gotten upset with you."

Something crossed his face then. Irritation, maybe. "Do not apologize."

The problem was, she *was* mad, and she couldn't ignore that. Because if anyone had been kind and supportive to her throughout all this, it was Grey. The guy she hadn't expected that from at all. She noted the uncertainty in his eyes. That, though, couldn't switch the sudden direction of her mind. It was like with all the emotion stuffed back and under control, logic took over.

At one time, this arrangement seemed okay because it was just sex for a few days. She could do that with Grey. No emotions, only raw, physical lust. But over the course of the weekend, things had changed.

She realized now that maybe they'd changed for her and not him. And that explained why she felt so burned. She was beginning to like Grey. A lot, it seemed. "I can't do this anymore."

"What can't you do?"

"This," she said, drawing on all her strength to ensure she kept talking. "I can't continue with this lie anymore. I mean, honestly, Grey, what are we doing here?"

He arched a single eyebrow. "We're enjoying each other, Evie. It's quite simple."

She'd heard what he said, but somehow she couldn't believe that anymore. "We enjoyed each other. But I've been fooling myself. Faking a relationship, that can't work." She moved into the closet and grabbed her suitcase. She knew what she had to do, as much as she'd known she had to leave Grand Rapids for Seattle. Because she'd always been that girl. Once she was decided on a plan, there was no stopping her.

When she returned to Grey and placed her suitcase on the bed, she continued, "Nothing good can come from this. You know it. I know it. We need to stop pretending."

"Evie," Grey said, more softly now. "You're upset, and that's completely understandable, but you're making this about us when it shouldn't be."

"But it *is* about us," she implored, unable to look at him, scared if she did, she'd lose her nerve. "This weekend was amazing, Grey. Honestly, maybe the happiest time in my life—"

His firm finger tucked under her chin, tilting her head up to meet his emotion-packed eyes. "Then what exactly is the problem?"

"The problem is that it's not real." She quickly moved away, aware of how easily she could lose herself in him and unzipped her suitcase.

"It's been a game, and you know that. You wanted to win, so you set up a scenario where you could, and I agreed because I didn't want to face Seth and Holly alone."

Grey visibly tensed, cursed, and folded his arms. "Why do women always have to make things so damn complicated?"

"Because we *are* complicated beings," Evie said, returning to the closet. She took all her clothes off the hangers then returned to her case, tossing them inside before grabbing her toiletries from the bathroom.

When she added those to the case, too, Grey hadn't moved an inch—he stood statue-still. "Why are you packing your bag?" Grey asked gruffly.

"I'm going to go stay with Holly."

"You don't need to do that," he stated, grabbing her hand. "We fly home tomorrow morning. There's no reason to change our plans because of what Holly and Seth are going through. Nothing has to change, Evie."

"Everything *has* changed." She ignored the way her skin sizzled at his touch and moved away from him. "The fact that I'm upset that you kept this from me means that I've changed. I can't put myself in a situation where I'm the kind of woman you told me about."

"What woman?"

"The woman who becomes too attached."

At his silence, the tension in the room grew thick and heavy. She took her undergarments from the dresser, feeling her throat tighten.

Grey's weighted voice came behind her. "I don't understand any of this, Evie. Why are you even thinking this? Yesterday was amazing. Why can't we continue where we stopped? Because I chose not to tell you about Seth's feelings for you? You're honestly that upset about that?"

"No, that's not what I'm upset about." She zipped up her suitcase, turning to him, laying her heart on the line. "I'm upset because you chose to think of how his feelings would affect your weekend over how they would affect me." She placed her suitcase on the floor and then rolled it behind her as she approached. "And you made that decision because this was only sex. That's okay. You don't owe me a damn thing." She paused, staring into his mesmerizing eyes and sighed. "You and I are not the same, Grey. We don't want the same things out of life. And that's okay, too. But I did this…" She lifted her chin and stated proudly, "I did this because I wanted you. I let myself believe that I could never care for you. But then you ended up being this amazing guy who surprised me in ways I totally wasn't expecting you to. And while those are the best kind of surprises, they're also dangerous."

Grey's nostrils flared, but that was the only indication that what she said even affected him.

She'd never been one to hide her feelings, and she knew she couldn't hide them now. "This weekend gave me more than you can even know. I feel like you helped me find my way back to myself, and for that, I'll always be grateful. But this, us continuing to pretend that this is real… it isn't good for me. In fact, it's setting me up to fail because I'll want things from you that I shouldn't."

With her heart screaming at her to stay, but her mind telling her to go, she stood up on her tiptoes and kissed his flexed jaw muscles. Determined she was making the right choice for herself, she took a step away from him then stopped, realizing she wasn't done yet. She glanced over her shoulder, and added, "You know what, Grey, I do believe in karma like you do," she explained. "I believe that we had this time together for a reason. You got me in the way you wanted me, and I found healing in the most unexpected way. That was our *thing*, and no one can ever take that away from us."

She moved to the door, and when she whisked it open, Grey's voice blistered. "Evie."

Her emotions in her throat, she turned back to him and waited for him to say *anything*…for him to ask her to stay because he wanted her there for more reasons than to only have her body.

She smiled softly at his silence and officially ended the fantasy. "Goodbye, Grey."

Chapter 12

Five days.

One hundred and twenty hours.

Seven thousand and two hundred minutes.

That's how long Grey had been trying to exist without Evie, and he'd been failing miserably. He had left Seattle one man and had come home another. Everything looked different around him. His life was unrecognizable. Where his world once seemed bright with optimism, now it appeared dull in comparison.

In his office, sitting behind his metal desk, he regarded the drafting table across the room, aware that there were clients to make happy. With taking the long weekend off from work unexpectedly, he was already days behind on a couple of projects. But new ideas weren't coming. He'd never been less inspired in his life. What seemed important before no longer mattered anymore, only Evie did.

She was everywhere, in his mind, even in his damn office, haunting him wherever he went. His thoughts kept circling back to her, again and again, chasing him. All he wanted to do was forget her and move on, and even that had been impossible to do.

He heaved a long sigh and turned in his chair, facing the bank of windows, glancing out at the city. Seattle's skyline had always inspired him. Some of the buildings climbing high into the clouds were his designs, and some were buildings that had been there for years. But this skyline was the reason he'd gotten into architecture.

When he went to his father's office every so often as a child, he'd been mesmerized by the lines of the buildings, the curves. They were perfect, like Evie's…

"Enough," he growled to himself, rising from his seat.

Though, even then, his gaze fell on the desk that Evie had used while she worked for his company. *Fuck, she won't leave me alone.* He pressed his fists against the table and breathed deeply, his chest tightening, muscles surging with adrenaline. He wasn't sure how much more of this punishment he could endure.

"Who pissed you off?"

When he slowly lifted his head and turned toward the doorway, he found his assistant, Janet, entering his office. Today, her short, blond bob was curled slightly, her fingernails painted a bright blue, matching the color of her fitted dress. "No one pissed me off," he said, shoving his hands into the pockets of his black slacks.

Janet's brows rose, her soft brown eyes searching his. "Mmhmm," was all she said as she stopped in front of his desk, a file folder in her hands. "Okay, well that's a lie, but let's move on. Your first meeting today is in an hour, which means we have the chance to talk about what's going on with you before you kick-start your day."

He leaned his back against the window and arched a brow at her.

"Do I look like I want to talk about it?"

She gave him a very thorough once-over then nodded. "Yes."

"No," he corrected.

She smirked, giving him that hard look she owned so well. "All right, so then let me clarify. You might not want to talk about it, but you should, because if you don't, you are going to explode and take your anger out on someone who doesn't deserve it."

While she had a point, Janet could be as intrusive as his mother, and he certainly didn't let his mother push him around. "Do you have a reason for coming in here, more than just to annoy me?" he asked.

"Of course, I do." She moved to the black, industrial chairs in front of his desk and took a seat before addressing him again. "We need to discuss something very serious, in fact."

"Which is?" he asked, thinking he didn't even want to know.

She crossed her legs, placing the folder on her lap and opening it, revealing papers. "I have the final check for Evie Richards here." She sorted through the file and pulled out a slip of paper. "While I could have asked someone in accounting to sign off on it, I wondered if you might like to deliver the check to her yourself."

Grey read between the lines and narrowed his eyes at her. The twinkle in the depths of hers sold her out. He moved to the front of his desk, resting against the edge and crossing his arms. "Janet, have you been spying on me?"

Her gaze lifted to the ceiling as she nibbled her lip. She finally said, "Spying sounds so harsh. I checked in on you."

He gave her a flat look. "And the difference between the two is…?"

"Well, originally, I was concerned when you decided to go on some random vacation completely out of the blue," she explained. "Which by the way is the first vacation you've been on since"—she pursed her lips, pondering—"actually, I can't recall a single time you've been on a personal trip since I started working here."

"That's because I haven't been on one," he confirmed.

She nodded as if her point had been proved. "Then I'm sure you can understand I was quite worried about you."

"What exactly were you afraid of?"

She held his stare. "That you'd joined a cult."

He chuckled. Her dramatics always amused him. "You do realize that in itself is crazy," he pointed out.

"It is not," she defended, hands pressing against the file folder. "People join cults all the time. One day, they are normal people. The next, they are giving away all their money and moving to remote areas never to be seen or heard from again."

"You thought that I would actually be that person?"

"Totally plausible," she said, eyes bright with conspiracies clearly running rampant in her mind. "So then, what kind of assistant and friend would I be not to make sure you weren't throwing your life away?"

He stared into her firm gaze and restrained his chuckle. "You watch too much television."

"Maybe." She half shrugged with a soft smile, leaning back in the chair. "But let's get back to the point. Because you were acting so unlike yourself, and out of concern for you, I checked on who were you were traveling with."

Janet would be privy to that information, too. She had total access to his life, including his credit cards because she organized his life for him and he implicitly trusted her. Regardless… "You could have asked me who I went with and I would have told you."

"Well, yes," she drawled, giving him a knowing look. "But what if you really had gone insane? You might have lied to me and given them all your money or something."

He stared at her blankly. "Do you honestly believe that I'm the type of man who would join a cult?"

"Weirder things have happened," she said, dead serious. "They happen every day, all over our country."

He snorted and shook his head at her. "I think it might be time to ban you from television. Soon, you'll have a secret room with conspiracy theories taped to the walls."

"Who says I don't already."

A long pause.

She gave a full belly laugh. "Just kidding. I'm not at that level yet, but I was concerned. Truly."

"Well, thank you for being worried, I do appreciate that." Janet had been with him long enough that she was like family, and he couldn't imagine his life without her. But that meant she was clingy like his mother. Always hounding him, always in his business, even if it was done out of love. "But I'm not in a cult, and I don't foresee joining one in the future either."

"Good," she said with a firm nod. "However, you still have a choice to make." She shook the check in her hand and added, "You can deliver this check to Evie yourself. Or you can stay in your office and keep pouting."

"I. Do. Not. Pout." He frowned.

"Oh, yeah?" She pointed at his face, a big smile on hers. "Pout. Scowl. Glare. Whatever way you want to look at it, you're miserable.

So instead of sitting in here and hating the world, go do something about it."

Grey glanced at the check in Janet's hand. His heart raced at the thought of seeing Evie again. He wanted to see her…touch her…taste her, of course, he did. But he'd done enough already to shove himself into Evie's life, and that hadn't ended well for her. Actually, it hadn't ended well for anyone.

From what the staff at the resort told him before he departed that same day to catch a private flight home, Holly cancelled her wedding. Grey wanted to know how Evie was holding up. But she hadn't come to him, called, texted…nothing. He wouldn't force her into anything again. His missing her was his punishment.

Determined in his next steps, he turned around to his desk and picked up a pen. Janet handed him the check, and after he'd signed it, he offered it back to her. "Send it by courier."

Janet's brows shot up, voice softened. "I think you're making a big mistake here."

"While I appreciate that you're looking out for me," he said slowly, ensuring she heard him. "I do not wish to discuss this any more than we have. That will be all, Janet."

Being the amazing assistant—and friend—she was, she nodded. "Yes, sir."

~

Only a few blocks away from Pike Place Market, Evie stood in the center of the bare room that would house a new up-and-coming media company that partnered with top brands to publish mobile apps and advertising. In three weeks, they'd leave behind their dingy office space and move into the elite downtown core of Seattle, where they'd make their mark on the world.

Evie studied the space. It was everything she'd hoped it would be and more. Bare white walls led down to dark barnwood floors, and above her, the industrial pipes had been left exposed. She'd been given a blank canvas to create the modern and fun environment the company was looking for, which she would give to them. And the project was precisely what she needed to get her head back in the game and off Grey.

She'd done the whole getting-over-a-guy routine before. Hell, she'd left Holly and Seth behind before, and had gotten past the hurt she felt with them. Surely, then, she could get over Grey. They barely had any history. One weekend. Plus, some working hours. That was it.

Yes, she was moving on already.

Determined to get her mind off things, she approached the bank of windows, staring out at another brick wall. While she liked the industrial feel of the building, the space didn't have the views that Grey's building…

Dammit, Evie, stop it!

She dropped her head into her hands and breathed deeply, then began rubbing her temples, trying desperately to erase Grey from her mind. He was there in her thoughts. All the time. Never fading. His touch. His voice. His smile. Those smoky eyes. Crap, even his cologne. She could forget nothing.

"Evie."

She gasped, startled, spinning around, finding her assistant, Monica, standing by the elevator with a hand on her hip. Her long, black hair framing her round face was perfectly in place as always. The tattoos covering her arms rocking. Even her cute, fifties-style cherry-print dress was normal. The concern on her face was anything but usual.

"Oh, my God," Evie said, laughing, pressing a hand to her thumping heart. "You scared the shit out of me."

"I said your name four times," Monica said with a smirk, approaching then and handing Evie a cup of coffee. "Is everything okay? You look frazzled."

"I'm fine." Evie sighed, accepting the cup. "Thanks for the coffee."

"No probs." Monica spun in a slow circle, taking in the open room as Evie had done. "Well, this space is pretty incredible, isn't it?"

Evie sipped her coffee and nodded. "I don't think we've ever worked on such a new space before."

"We haven't," Monica agreed, glancing toward the bank of windows before adding, "Do we have total control of the design?"

"Total freedom with the elements," Evie explained, hugging her paper cup with both hands, embracing the warmth. "But they're pretty strict on wanting a modern design with a retro flare."

Monica blinked. "They want modern but retro?"

"Yes." Evie laughed.

"People are so confusing," Monica muttered, shaking her head.

"I can't disagree with you there." Evie scanned the space again, sipping her coffee, imagining all the modern furniture with a couple of retro accents to give the clients the vibe they wanted. "But I actually think what they want is going to work in this space," she finished.

"You're the expert," Monica said, then she practically purred, "When do we get to go shopping?"

"Later today."

"Oh, goodie!"

Evie laughed at the gleam in Monica's eyes. Sure, Monica was damn good at keeping the schedule organized and the clients happy, but her eyes lit up whenever they started on a new project, all because they got to spend other people's money. Monica had a full-fledged shopping addiction, and she'd made a career out of it.

"So," Monica drawled, shifting from foot to foot. "There's something else we need to talk about."

Evie swallowed the coffee in her mouth. "What's that?"

"Greyson Crawford's…" Instinctively, Evie froze as Monica added, "…firm delivered our final payment before I left the office." She reached into her purse and handed Evie the check. "Looks like Grey signed it himself."

Evie ran her fingers across Grey's signature. Every check before this one had always been signed by the CFO of his company or someone else in accounting. Why did he sign this check himself?

Was he thinking about me? Did he want me to know that I had been on his mind? Does that mean something? Or is this just a check that he signed?

Round and round Evie went. Back and forth her mind returned to him, no matter how many times she told herself to get over it. Her heart squeezed, her soul feeling empty without him. And the power of that admission to herself was simply staggering. She barely knew him. They only had three days and a few hours of an additional night together. What if they had longer, would this need for him get worse or fade away?

She drew in a deep breath then lifted her head and smiled, handing Monica back the check. "Well, that's done then."

Monica tucked the check away in her purse and then regarded Evie for a long moment. "Is it done, though?" she asked softly. "Because from where I'm sitting, and judging by how sad you've been since you came home from your trip, it seems anything but done."

Evie hesitated, staring at a woman who'd become her best friend over the last years of working together. She tried to clear her mind of all the messy emotions, making this simple, sticking to the facts. "Do you think it's weird that I miss him?"

"Weird, hell no," Monica said with a laugh. "He's tattoos, sex, and alpha yumminess. Also, let's not forget that you said he gave you the best sex of your life. I think anyone would miss *that*."

If only it were that easy. "But it's not the sex that I miss," Evie explained, trying to get out what she felt so she could begin to understand it herself. "It's all of him. It's the way I felt around him. It's how comfortable I was with him." Emotions began to tighten her throat, but she pushed them away, feeling like now that she'd started talking, she couldn't stop. "I miss how happy I was with him, how content I felt, how easy life seemed when I was with him. Is that normal for me to feel that way?"

"Frankly, I think you're asking the wrong person if you want to know about normal relationships," Monica said, shifting the straps of her purse higher on her shoulder. "Greg and I had a shotgun wedding after a month of dating when I was nineteen."

"But you're still together and happy, so I think that makes you entirely qualified to answer that question."

Monica gave a lopsided smile. "Maybe." She drew in a deep breath before speaking again. "If I know anything about love, it's that it's hard to find that special someone who makes you light up inside. If Greyson

Crawford made that happen for you, then I say go and tell him and see where it goes."

"Easier said than done," Evie said aloud this time, dropping down onto the floor to sit cross-legged. "If he wanted something more," she stated, as Monica sat down across from her, "he could have said: 'I want to give this a real shot.' But he didn't."

"Okay, that's a valid point," Monica agreed, setting the skirt of her dress over her knees. "Though maybe this is all as complicated for him as it is for you."

"You could be totally right about that," Evie agreed with a soft nod, placing her coffee mug between her crossed legs. "But I've been hurt enough. It was scary to start dating again after Seth. The thought of opening my heart to a guy like Grey outright terrifies me."

Monica paused then nodded. "Love is risky. Scary as fuck, really." Her head tilted, her eyes narrowed in concentration. "However, what if he's really never found that *one,* and that's why he's been so closed up. I mean, it sounded like you two had something incredible. Magic like that only happens once."

Evie glanced down at her coffee cup and sighed heavily, thinking that's exactly what Violet had told her, too.

"For as long as I've known you," Monica added softly, breaking into the silence. "You've never been the type to sit around and mope. So, what are you going to do?"

She smiled and offered, "Drink to get over him?"

"Oh, hell yes, it is Friday night, after all." Monica slapped Evie's leg, her eyes twinkling with ideas for the adventure ahead of them. "Let's get this shit done here so we can get shit-faced."

"Deal," Evie said with a laugh.

Tomorrow would come, and the next day, and hopefully each day that passed, she'd miss him less until she forgot the name: Greyson Crawford.

Chapter 13

The following afternoon, with laughter gliding through the air, Grey moved to the cooler next to the grill. Earlier in the morning, he'd received a call inviting him to join Maddox and his wife, Joss, for a backyard party at the house on Lake Washington that Maddox inherited after his father passed. The company alone would have brought him here, but the chance to drink sounded all too good right then.

Every year, Maddox held this event to welcome the new rookies into his division at the Seattle Police Department in the west precinct. Now that Maddox was the captain in the east precinct and had been for the last year, his party was still for the rookies, but it had grown in size since he invited the entire department now. Sure, Grey wasn't a cop and therefore a total outsider here, but he never missed a party, and no one ever seemed to mind that he came. Though even if they did have a problem with him being there, no one would dare question Maddox.

When Grey finally reached the cooler, he grabbed a cold beer. His body ached from his head to his toes. Exhaustion weighed heavily on him, slowly swallowing him up, and not even a run this morning or jerking his cock in the shower after had done anything to get his head right.

I still miss her.

Every hour only deepened the void of Evie's absence.

Each minute seemed longer than the last.

A small breeze picked up, bringing the greasy scent of the hamburgers on the grill when he cracked open the beer. He tossed the cap into the beer case next to the cooler then scanned the crowd, his gaze falling on Joss. Back in the day, he couldn't imagine Maddox loving any woman hard enough to marry her. Now, he couldn't imagine seeing his friend without Joss next to him.

Her long, chocolate-brown hair rested on her shoulder, while she held onto the hands of her little girl, Sofia, who wobbled her way forward, having just begun to walk. Thoughts of Evie passed through his mind. *She'd look so pretty holding a sweet baby like that...*

He grunted, shook his head, and took a big gulp of his beer. Fuck, what the hell was wrong with him?

When he lowered his brew, he found Joss watching him, her light green eyes piercing into his as usual. He gave her a soft smile, which she returned, even if her brows furrowed a little—a look she'd been giving him since he came back from Punta Cana. An expression that told him he appeared even worse than he thought. *Great.*

"Better be careful, people might start believing you're actually boring."

Grey snorted and glanced over his shoulder, finding Maddox. He cupped his friend's shoulder, asking with a smirk, "Am I not being social enough for your liking?"

"A ghost would be friendlier." Maddox gestured toward the pathway next to the patio bar surrounded by big evergreens. "Let's get away for a minute."

The look on Joss's face a moment ago, matched with the tension in Maddox's expression now told Grey all he needed to know. "Let me guess, Joss thinks you need to talk to me?"

"Yes," Maddox said, his look one of exasperation. "She thinks you're depressed and in dire need of help. So, being the good friend I am, we're going to have a talk that neither of us wants to have so that I look like the most fabulous husband—which I also am."

"Well, in that case"—Grey chuckled dryly and waved out toward the pathway—"lead the way."

Maddox grinned and gave Joss a firm nod, clearly telling her he had Grey handled.

Grey snorted and followed behind, passing by the partygoers standing near the patio bar with the dark wooden stools. Soon, he stepped into the thick forest, and he stayed on Maddox's heels. He followed behind on the thin trail that finally stopped at a bench, offering a stunning view of Lake Washington, with his mother's mansion far off in the distance on the right side.

Maddox took a seat first, then Grey dropped down next to him, stretching out his legs, crossing one ankle over the other, gazing out at the quiet water. A few boats were out on the lake, some people swimming on the other side of the shore.

"Joss thinks I should be worried about you," Maddox eventually said, breaking the silence. Elbows on his knees, he glanced sideways at Grey, clear concern in his expression. "Should I be?"

"Worried?" Grey pondered then shook his head. "No."

Maddox snorted. "You neither look nor sound convincing."

Grey tossed back another big gulp of his beer, savoring the citrusy hints. "Evie, she's…" He paused, voice thick, so he cleared his throat before continuing. "She's gotten right in here." He tapped his temple.

One brow arched, Maddox asked, "And why exactly is that a bad thing?"

"Because she ended it."

"When?"

"I flew home from the Dominican without her." Grey paused, trying to sort through all the shit in his head.

"I'm confused. When we talked, things seemed good," Maddox said. "What happened?"

"The wedding we went there for fell apart, and I think that rattled her." There were too many details to share about Evie's past with Holly and Seth, and they weren't his details to share. "Evie…she's been through a lot…too much."

Maddox regarded Grey, sipping his beer, then said, "So then unrattle her."

"Again, seems simple," Grey said, admitting a truth that had been circling around in his head. "But I can't risk hurting her by accident. I can't be responsible for seeing a woman that is entirely good, so fucking sweet, hurt again."

A gleam formed in Maddox's eyes, and the side of his mouth arched. "You're worried about fucking this up, and I've never seen you concerned about that before with anyone. You've actually cultivated your life so there's no chance you will fuck up with women because they always know the score. And yet here you are. I think that says a lot, don't you?"

"I know exactly what it says and what it means," Grey said, not doubting how special Evie was. That was undeniable, and it was a truth in his mind he could no longer run from. "But I'm not thinking about myself in all this, I'm thinking about her. She's good in ways I didn't know a person could be. She loves unconditionally. She's warm to those who don't deserve it, and yet she's strong in front of them." He tapped his temple again. "So as much as she's in here, I can't chase her again when she left wanting nothing more to do with me."

"I do understand that," Maddox said softly, and the trees standing tall behind him rustled with the breeze, "but you're fucking miserable, so how is this the right solution either?"

"Thus my current problem." Grey hesitated, then he allowed the emotion to fill his expression and his voice. "I went after her in the first place for my own selfish reasons. I won't do that again. She left, I never stopped her. End of story."

Maddox's expression softened, obviously now understanding the weight of all this. He glanced out at the water for a few minutes, sipping his beer. "Perhaps you're looking at this all wrong," he finally said, turning to Grey again, awareness in his eyes. "She's fearful of getting close to the Greyson Crawford she knew before—the love 'em and leave 'em guy. You proved her right by not demanding she stay. But you're no longer that guy. Have you told her that?"

Grey frowned. "No, but it's too late to take that back. The damage has already been done."

"It's never too late." Maddox drew in a long, deep breath, leaning back against the bench before explaining, "Even I can see that your perspective has changed. Believe me, I understand that outlook because I've experienced it myself. But it's Evie that's caused this shift in your life, made you doubt things you've never questioned before. With her, things are right. Without her, things are wrong. It truly is that simple."

"I understand that she's the reason I feel unsteady," Grey admitted. "But—"

Maddox cupped Grey's shoulder, giving a measured look. "Here's some unsolicited advice from a friend. If she's got you this caught up, I'd say you know all you need to. From where I'm sitting, it's simple: go and get her. If she left, it was because she was protecting herself. Be the man she wants you to be."

Be the man she wants you to be...

Grey pondered that, and from where Maddox sat, that would be the logical answer. Grey knew it wouldn't be enough. "But I talked her into agreeing to something she never should have before—"

"Well, this time, don't talk her into it," Maddox said, eyes bright. "Ask her."

I'M OFF TO *find my happy nook. I'll reach out soon.*

Evie lowered down onto her porch swing at her two-story house in the Squire Park neighborhood, with its light gray siding and cherry-red front door, and smiled at the text from Holly. With her cell phone in her hand, and her landline against her ear, she said to Allison Richards, her mother, "Holly just texted me. Has she gone somewhere or something?"

If anyone had the town gossip, it was her mother. "From what I heard," Allison replied in her soft, soothing voice, "she's taking a sabbatical to rediscover herself and traveling Europe for the next six months, or at least that's what Pam"—Holly's mother—"told me."

"Wow, good for her," Evie said, putting her cell to sleep and placing it on the white floorboards beneath her bare feet. "I remember all during high school, Holly wanted to do that. I'm happy for her," she finished, truly meaning that.

Whatever peace she and Holly needed to come to, they got that in the tropics. Maybe it'd been the long talk they had the night before the wedding, or possibly because Holly didn't marry Seth, but the healing had started between them. Her friendship with Holly would never be what it once was, though Evie wasn't ready to give up on it entirely either. History between people meant something.

"Truthfully," Allison said dryly. "I think you might be the only one who feels happy for Holly. Seth's family is furious. And Holly's parents aren't thrilled either. But they'll recover, and in the end, it seems that Holly's wanted to get out of Grand Rapids for a long time. A broken heart was just the push she needed to find herself."

"And how about Seth?" Evie asked, considering his feelings, too. Holly wasn't the only one that Evie could forgive. But Seth and she didn't have the closeness that Evie had with Holly, a special friendship that came from someone who truly knew you. "Do you think he'll be okay?"

"I'm sure he'll be fine," Allison quipped. "Men are resilient. One second, Evie." She hesitated, and that's when Evie heard beeping in the background telling her that her mom was working at the hospital today.

"Yes. Yes," Allison said to someone obviously in the room with her. "Yes, that's fine. Give me another few minutes, and I'll be there." When she spoke again, her professional voice vanished, and her soft voice filled the phone line. "And you, my darling, how are you? I can't imagine any of this has been easy on you."

Evie sighed, anticipating what was to come. Her mom was about to go full therapist on her. She couldn't help it. Job hazard. "To be perfectly honest, I'm not even sure how I feel about it all. It's been a bit of a whirlwind. I'm still processing, I think."

"That's understandable," Allison replied, and clearly shut a door since the background noise faded away. "Maybe you're a little sad for them that it didn't work. Maybe you're also a little happy that they failed. It's perfectly normal to feel both ways."

Evie waved at her neighbors Todd and Phillip, who walked their French bulldog, Dixie, down the sidewalk. "Is that the therapist answer or the mom answer?" she asked.

"It's both," Allison said without hesitation. "You all have a lot of history together. If you can get past this with Holly and move on to settle into a new friendship between you, then wonderful. But it's also okay to cut ties and think of yourself in all this, too. They both hurt you, deeply."

Evie drew in a long, deep breath, not sure how she'd survive without her mother. She always felt put together because she'd grown up around a seriously put-together and strong woman. While she was a little more logical than her mother would like, she never felt alone in this big, crazy world. She always felt understood, and there was something magical in that. "Thanks, Mom. I'm sure I'll be fine once the dust settles."

"Good. So, now that we've got that out of the way," her mother said, voice turning hard. "Who is Greyson Crawford?"

Evie stared at the house across the street. *Fuck.* "Well...I..." She kind of hoped her parents wouldn't find out about Grey. Damn close-knit communities! "I haven't mentioned him because I wasn't really expecting it to work out," she explained gently. "He just came to the wedding with me. I didn't want you to go all therapist on me and examine the hell out of him."

Her mother paused. Then, "You want me to believe that you, Evie Richards, took a man you don't really like to your childhood friend's wedding?"

"Yes."

Another hesitation then she gave a curt snort. "Evie, I read people for a living. That's my job. Do you honestly think that I don't know you're lying to me right now?"

"Oh, I know you know," Evie retorted, pushing against her feet so the swing began to move back and forth. "I'm just hoping you won't say anything about it."

Allison laughed softly. "You are your father's daughter, there is no doubt about that."

Dad hated talking feelings with Mom, too. A little hope appeared. "Does that mean we don't have to talk about this?" Evie asked.

"No," her mother said. "You're sad. I can hear it in your voice. What's wrong?"

"Nothing is wrong. I'm not sad. Maybe a little confused." She hesitated, and then knew better. "Okay, maybe very confused, but honestly, I'm fine."

"Evie," her mother drawled.

A shiver ran down Evie's spine. She knew that voice. If she didn't tell her mother something, she'd be there on the next plane. Because as much as her mom could poke and prod, she did so because she was worried. Maybe her job caused that panic. She knew all the terrible things that could go on in someone's mind.

To kill her mother's concern, and looking for comfort from the one person who absolutely never judged her, she explained, "Everything is a mess. And, yes, his name is Greyson Crawford, but everyone calls him Grey. You'd like everything about him, Mom. He's an architect here in Seattle. Actually, scratch that, I'm pretty sure you'd love him. He's sweet and charming and funny and strong. But he's got major commitment issues that you, better than anyone, knows can't be fixed unless the person wants to fix them."

"Commitment issues how? Like he runs when things get emotional?"

Evie sighed again, tipping her head back against the edge of the swing, the wind brushing across her face. "Well, to be honest, I'm the one who ran, but it's because I know the type of guy he is."

"What type?"

"Love 'em and leave 'em."

Evie lifted her head, watching a bird fly by and land on her big maple tree in her front yard, as her mother commented, "So, you left him before he could leave you?"

"Maybe." Evie dropped her head into her hand. "Was that wrong? Did I make a huge mistake?"

"There's nothing that can't be undone as long as you're honest with yourself and with everyone else. What happened with Holly and Seth would have rattled anyone, and for you, it would be amplified because of your past with Seth. It is understandable that in that moment you would be uncertain about anyone's intentions toward you."

Evie sighed. "He's…it's intense with him…no, it's terrifying."

"Scary isn't always a bad thing, sweetheart. Being afraid means you're feeling something and being pushed out of your comfort zone. It means that he could hurt you, but that means your heart is opening to him in a way that could be a very good thing in the end."

"But where do I even start?" Evie asked softly. *How do I fix all this?*

"Start with honesty and go from there."

Seemed like the only place she could begin. "I love you, Mom."

"I love you, too." She paused again. "I'm sorry, but patients call. Good luck with this. You're a beautiful, sweet, and amazing woman. Trust your gut, Evie."

"Thanks, I will. Bye."

"Goodbye."

Evie clicked end on her cordless phone and then placed it down beside her cell phone on the porch. With the birds chirping and the wind rustling the leaves on the tree, she leaned her head back against the swing and shut her eyes. "Okay, Evie, think this through," she said to herself. "Is this more than sex? He did fight hard to go out with you. Can he commit to a woman? Who knows, you didn't really give him a chance. Can he care about you? He made you so happy. Dammit, Evie, you should've at least stayed to talk. He made you happy!"

Someone cleared their throat.

Evie screamed, finding Grey leaning against the porch. He arched a single brow, giving her a sly grin. "Done talking to yourself, angel?"

Chapter 14

Grey fought back a smile at the way Evie's cheeks flushed a deep crimson. Sure, his arrival surprised her, but he liked surprising her. The sweetness in her expression, the happiness that someone cared enough *to* surprise her. Fuck yeah, he'd chase down the opportunity to see this look on her again. And for the first time in days, he finally felt steady again.

While he'd listened to her talk to herself, he had regarded her house a little. He never imaged a house suiting a person completely, but hers did, and he guessed that was because she was an interior designer. All the little touches, like the pillows with the hearts on the swing, to the *Home Sweet Home* welcome mat at the front door, held an Evie flair. He liked this house. A lot. Though he liked the gaping woman sitting motionless on the swing even more.

After taking a moment to obviously recover, she cleared her throat. "Um, you weren't supposed to hear that conversation."

"I beg to differ," he said with an arched brow. "Those thoughts were about me. Who better to hear them?"

She blinked twice. "Why are you here?"

"To talk to you, if that's all right."

She paused, then gave a sweet smile and a little shrug. "Well, you came all this way, so I guess so."

All the tension in his chest faded just that easily. It was in her smile, in the warmth of her eyes, in all of her, he found his comfort. Keeping his eyes fixed on her, he moved to where he wanted to go. To her.

As he climbed her porch steps, she sat up a little straighter on the swing, bending her legs, bringing her knees to her chest. He took his time and then dropped next to her, needing to get this right. Staring out at the road, he used his feet to push the swing back and forth, but finally, with her near, his mind calmed.

"I'm sorry that I hurt you, Evie," he started, tackling the most important thing first. "Keeping how Seth felt from you was because of my own insecurity." He turned to her, her gaze locked onto his. "I knew I only had that one weekend with you, and I didn't want to taint what we had going. Of course, my plan backfired." He liked how softly she stared at him, any anger she had for him was clearly gone now, so he added, "My intention was never to hurt you. In fact, I wanted to make you happy."

"You did make me happy," she said, resting her cheek on her knee. "But I also don't think you're the only one who needs to apologize. I overreacted. I shouldn't have left you like that, and that was *my* insecurity. You had no obligation to tell me about what Seth said to you. And, honestly, I'm not even upset about that anymore. It was a knee-jerk reaction."

"It was an honest response," he retorted, knowing that mistake on his part could never be corrected. "I should have done more than just told you about him. I should have laid him out, staking my claim to you right then and there."

She lifted her brows. "And what would that have accomplished?"

"It would have told him that you're mine. It would have shown you that I wanted you. That I'd fight for you. That I'd be all that you need and more."

She paused, her eyes searching his. "Is that what I am...*yours?*"

"Well, you see," he said with a smile, pushing his feet again, sending the swing rocking back and forth. "That's what brings me here." He drew in a long, deep breath, collecting his thoughts before addressing her again. "You have to understand, Evie, that it's just been me for thirty-five years. I formed habits, I guess. I've gotten used to the way things are in my life."

After another gentle push of the swing, he added, "I think along the way, it was a conscious choice I made. To be and stay single. I liked my life that way. It became simplified, comfortable, uncomplicated." He smiled then, and using his free hand, he brushed his knuckles across her jawline. "Then you came along and turned my simple world upside down." He liked how her eyes fluttered shut when he cupped her cheek, and how she leaned into his touch. It made him know he was right where he should be. "Those three days with you were the best days of my life."

She gave her sweet smile. "For me, too."

With those few words, his world realigned, making him feel centered again. Yet this new world revolved around the woman before him. "It's been six days since I came home. Six painful fucking days that I haven't had you in my arms. I can't endure another moment of it."

Whether it was his words or his expression, he didn't know, but it made her act. She wrapped her arms around his neck, and he pulled her in close to straddle his waist. Dropping his head into her neck, he inhaled, taking in her flowery perfume, keeping hold of her in a way he'd never needed to grasp onto anything before.

He stayed there, time passing them by, and him not counting the minutes. These past days had broken him. Ruined him. And now, having her back, nice and close, was all that he needed and more.

Eventually, though, she moved away, and he slid his hands up and down her arms, keeping that connection. Her smile returned, tears in her eyes, when she said, "You're not alone in feeling like you came back to Seattle a different person."

"Explain."

Staying on his lap, facing him, she threaded her fingers with his. "You have to understand, Grey," she cleverly used his words back on him. "I thought I had it all figured out. I've always been the bigger person. I'm the one who forgives first. I'm the one who takes hit after hit because I'm strong enough to take it and survive. Then you came along and turned my world upside down."

The strength...the sparkle...Christ, she was *his*. "How did I change things?" he asked, stroking his finger across her thumb.

"You made me run," she said softly. "I never run, not from anyone. You made me worry about giving you my heart, and I know that's because you could devastate me in ways that Seth never could, because with you...it's *real*."

"I won't hurt you," he murmured, squeezing her fingers.

"That's a promise you can't make," she retorted, squeezing his hand back. "No matter how hard you try, people get hurt. It happens. But we can promise each other that we'll always try and make sure we remember the other person's feelings. That we'll stay and do everything we can to work out the hard stuff. That we'll protect each other. That we'll always choose love."

"I can do that," he told her. "Can you?"

"I can." She hesitated again, this time longer, and when she spoke again, her voice was thick with emotion. "I want you to know that I felt more loved by you in three days than I felt in years with Seth. I don't want to pretend that doesn't mean anything. It's been awful without you."

"Now that, angel, is something I completely understand." His chest constricted, and his throat tightened too, but he pushed through it all, keeping his feet planted on the floorboards to stop the swing from moving. "And that's probably the perfect lead-in to what I have to ask next."

Her eyebrows winged up, curiosity filling her expression.

He began, "First, I didn't understand how you could forgive Holly and Seth. It simply didn't make sense to me, but I know now that's because I didn't see that you honestly have no control over who you fall in love with. I always thought it was a choice, and I chose not to elect that with anyone." He paused, knowing he had to get this right, "Then you came along, and I realized I don't control shit. I still can't say I'll be perfect at this, or that I won't fuck up along the way, but all I know is that I hate not being with you. So, Evie, shall we continue what we started in the tropics?"

Her mouth twitched. "Are you asking me to be your first girlfriend, Greyson Crawford?"

"I am."

She hesitated for a long moment, her eyes searching his before she smiled. "Yes, Grey, I'll be your first girlfriend." Another pause then laughed softly, eyes twinkling unlike anything he'd seen from her before. "Oh my, God, I'm popping your relationship cherry."

He narrowed his eyes at her, watching her gaze flare with desire. "That sounds like you don't think I'll stick."

"No, I think you'll stick, but I am going to have to teach you a lot."

He released her hands and dragged his thumb across her bottom lip, infatuated with that damn mouth. "Dare I say that sounds like a challenge."

She grinned sensually. "Maybe it is."

"Well, angel, I happen to like challenges. Particularly when they involve getting naked."

Chapter 15

The front door slammed behind them, and Evie gasped as her back hit the wall, Grey's kiss becoming all consuming. The heat of his mouth moved to her neck, and he devoured her flesh, his hands moving to her bottom where he squeezed. For the first time since she returned to Seattle, beneath his hands, her world realigned. This, *him*, she wanted to give this a real shot. She moaned, melting into the way he took command of her body so easily, heating her up, making her want him with full-on desperation.

She pushed him forward, playing the push and pull she knew Grey enjoyed, and he gripped her arms. With a grin on his face, he pushed her back against the wall, pinning her there. Her thighs clenched, her sex becoming drenched with the way he watched. The way he handled her with a firm confidence that made all thoughts disappear. Heat flooded her as his mouth returned to hers, more forcefully than before. He angled his head, deepening the kiss, and she gave in to all that he wanted from her and more.

His deep grunt vibrated against her skin, causing her to shiver. With a final swirl of his tongue, he leaned away, stripping his shirt off in one quick move, and her hands came to his chest, stroking the heat of his skin, the valleys of his hard muscles, flexing beneath her fingers. He unbuckled his belt then opened his pants, taking down the zipper, and then he boldly grabbed her hand, guiding her to where he wanted her.

With his smoky, seductive eyes on her, she eagerly stroked him, loving the way his hips shot forward and his expression intensified. Each deep moan he gave, the thickness of his cock, the hardness of him made her want all of him. His pupils were dilated, and his expression shone with sinful intentions. She squeezed his thick shaft, urging him on.

He responded instantly and grunted. "Fuck, that's good, angel."

She shivered against the promise of his voice, needing more of him, wanting to be all that he desired and more. "Let me taste you," she whispered, letting her voice be heard in the way she knew he liked.

A low growl rose from his throat, and he placed a hand around her neck, not tight enough to frighten, but firmly enough to keep her pinned against the wall, those smoldering eyes stripping her bare as the seconds dragged on. With a dark smile, he reached for her shirt, yanking it off quickly then he had the rest of her clothes off a split second later.

She went to reach for his chest again, needing oh-so-desperately to be connected to him. He grabbed both of her wrists and murmured, "Have your taste."

God, that *look*…his voice…the power he exuded…she'd never experienced a man like him. Grey knew his worth. He also knew how to command women. But it was different with her, she knew that. She felt it in the way he looked at her, as if they were completely connected, as if she were the only woman to ever captivate him like this. He made her feel desired and loved all at once.

She squatted, keeping her back pressed against the wall as he thrust his jeans and boxer briefs down to his knees. She took hold of his thick cock in front of her face and held him at the base, sucking him deeply into her mouth. He tossed his head back and moaned, and she sucked harder, pulling in her cheeks around him before rubbing her lips up and down over his shaft. Teasing aside, she pleasured him, sliding her tongue across the slit, tasting the saltiness of his pre-cum as she inhaled his musky, masculine scent.

Grey was pure man. All delicious male. She couldn't get enough.

She glanced up at him, finding his one hand pressed against the wall, his head bowed, gaze on her. "You're so fucking sexy, Grey," she told him, swirling her tongue over his cockhead.

Whether it was what she said or how she said it, his expression suddenly changed, becoming more serious, more feral. Not a second later, she was on her feet again and spun around, her cheek against the wall. His hand pressed against the back of her neck, then he was kissing his way down her body, and she was shivering in anticipation.

With a low growl vibrating deep into her core, he grabbed her hips, pulling them out and kicking her legs apart, spreading her wide. She gasped as his tongue suddenly licked her sex from behind. In those same moments, she heard rustling, could tell he was grabbing a condom out of his wallet. His tongue continued to slide deliciously across her hot slit, and she pushed back against him, wanting more, needing more.

She shut her eyes against the pleasure, and then she was trembling as he squeezed both her cheeks, opening her wider for his tongue. Over and over again, he licked her, readying her.

Just as her moans became higher pitched, he was there, his chest pressed against her back. With one hand on her neck, and the other on her hip, he entered her right to the hilt, filling her, pleasing her.

"Fuck," she breathed, her eyes pinching shut against the perfection of him.

His deeper growl sounded at her back when he began pumping his hips, not slow and sensual, but hard and demanding, a claim that she read in each of his punishing thrusts. She screamed against the force building inside her, ready to blow. Though he clearly had other ideas than a quick fuck to a hard orgasm because he withdrew right as she peaked in her climax.

"Where's your bedroom?" he murmured in her ear.

"Upstairs," she wheezed.

He spun her around, and she met his grin seconds before she found herself tossed over his shoulder. A hard slap on her ass later, followed by his deep chuckle, he headed up the staircase and entered the small bedroom with her queen-size bed and white metal headboard.

He slid her down the heat of his body until she stood before him, and told her, "Go get your vibrator."

She blinked. "How do you know I have a vibrator?"

One brow arched, and he repeated, "Go get your vibrator."

She gave a soft laugh and rolled her eyes, though she moved to her closet. There, she grabbed the box on the shelf, and she reached inside. When she turned back to him, she held up the black wand vibrator, offering it to him.

"No, angel, let me watch you."

Her breath hitched at this new game. She saw it in the way the side of his mouth arched. He was playing on her voyeuristic kink, and she fully intended to play along. Wicked heat coursed through her when she moved to her bed, sat on the edge, and turned the vibe onto a medium speed, placing it on her clit. The immediate buzz had her eyes shutting, and her breath slowly escaped her. She forced herself to look at him, and when she did, she lost her breath altogether.

Grey stood at the end of the bed, his hand around the base of his cock, keeping the condom in place, and he stroked himself. *Dear God.* A rapid flush of heat followed by a deep shiver stormed over her. The vibrator buzzed against her clit, tickling her into a higher pleasure, but it was *him* creating the blistering burn inside.

He stared at her intently with those smoky, passionate eyes, pinning her to the bed without a single hand on her body. Emotions charged the air between them, and she reached up, tugging on her nipple, needing more intensity. She moaned and shuddered, easily losing herself in the passion that shone in the depths of his eyes. But it was the small, sly smile he gave her—like he knew how much he owned her—that sent her head back, chin pointing to the ceiling, and her body shaking with her orgasm.

When she recovered and lifted her head, he gripped the base of his cock, his squared chest flexed, the lines of his six-pack more defined than ever. "You had your turn. Now I want mine. Do you want me to fuck you, Evie?"

"Yes."

His sizzling gaze held hers. "Beg me," he murmured.

She finally breathed again, near gasping now, seeing the promise in his eyes that he'd give her pleasures she'd never known. "Please, I want you...I need you."

"No." He stepped in between her spread legs, gazing at her bare breasts before looking her in the eye again. "I don't want to hear it from your mouth...*show* me...." He dragged a thumb across her bottom lip, and in that second, she felt every barrier she'd ever put in place come tumbling down under the strength of his touch. She didn't need to worry with him. She could let go.

She felt her heart soften as she leaned forward and sucked on his thumb.

His eyes flared with heady heat. "Yeah, angel, that's what I want. Give me everything." He grabbed her legs and pulled her bottom to the edge of the bed. But before he entered her, he reached down next to the bed for something.

When he straightened again, she noticed a couple of clothespins in his hand, clearly from the laundry basket she'd brought in earlier after drying her clothes on the line. Instantly, she went to sit up.

"Stay there," he said, pressing a hand against her chest, keeping her on the bed. He laid the clothespins on the mattress and then took the vibrator, turning it up to the highest speed then placed it on her clit. "Hold this right here for me. Do not remove it," he said with a smirk. "Do you understand?"

"Yes." She gasped and trembled.

He glanced around her room for a moment. It became near impossible to watch him when he moved to her dresser, the pleasure nearly blinding her. Only when he returned to her did she notice he had one of her fashion scarves in his hands. She anticipated him binding her, she felt the sensation ripple across her wrist.

He surprised her, like he always seemed to do, by placing the scarf over her eyes. He tied a tight knot at the back of her head, obstructing her view. She wasn't bathed in darkness, but it was like a curtain had been placed over her eyes, leaving only shadows visible.

Silence fell.

In those seconds, she became aware of so much more. Her heavy breathing, the sounds coming from outside, even Grey's breathing in front of her. But more, she could feel his presence, the strength he exuded. Goose bumps rose across her flesh, the hair on her arms standing up as he slid his warm hands up her thighs.

She exhaled deeply as he leaned over her, swirling his tongue around one of her puckered nipples. She kept the vibrator against her sex, buzzing delightfully on her bundle of nerves, and she gasped when she felt the tip of his cock at her entrance. When he fully entered her, she released a ravenous moan she didn't even recognize, while he slowly shifted his hips in and out. His wet, strong mouth sealed across her other nipple, teasing the bud into a tight knot.

Then she knew why.

Soon, his mouth was gone, and she felt a squeeze on her nipple, tightening and tightening while he applied the clothespin…until she gritted her teeth against the painful pinch. Once he released the clothespin, leaving it there on her nipple, his hand came down on the vibrator, and the pleasure brought her focus there. He moved his hips faster now, working into a fast rhythm, as her other nipple endured the pinch of the clothespin.

This time, the pain never came, the buzz on her clit had her gasping and moaning and unable to think about anything else, as it began to feel like hands were touching her clit, inside her, her nipples. The thickness of his cock rammed into her, and she gripped the bed sheets, feeling so full, so taken, when suddenly she felt a sensation new to her.

His damp thumb pressed against her anus, gently applying pressure, until with a *pop* he slipped inside her. He kept this thumb there, and every new sensation blasted through her, leaving her mindless. The tightness on her nipples. The torturous buzzing on her clit, squeezing her eyes shut tight. His hard cock filling her up, riding her hard. And the fullness of his thumb, making her feel touched in ways no one ever dared to touch her before.

With a roar, she arched her back, taken higher and higher.

In that very moment, he yanked the blindfold down, placing it around her neck. She forced her eyes open, finding dominance hovering over her. Grey's eyes were intense, his muscles flexed, as he took what was *his*.

That very statement echoed in the air around them as he took one of her hands and placed it on his chest, then did the same with the other. That's when she knew why he bound women. Emotion rushed across his face, and *this*, running her hands up his chest, cupping his face, and staring at him intimately was something he saved for her. For the only women who touched his heart. It never needed to be said or ever explained. It was their secret, the one thing she knew about him that no one else did.

And it was in that moment that she gave Grey what he wanted. Her heart.

With all that emotion burning between them, her breathing hitched, her climax...*right there*. And in that very second, with quick hands, Grey removed the clothespins. Then there was nothing but pleasure in its purest and rawest form as she lost herself in the intensity that he offered her, hearing her screams echoing his roars.

Sometime later, when her mind decided to work again, Grey's soft chuckle brushed across her. "Fuck, you came so hard you made me come with you."

Only then did Evie open her eyes to realize Grey was resting on top of her with the vibrator now lying on the mattress, still buzzing away. It was a statement of how hard she came that she couldn't remember him dropping down onto her or when she exactly let go of the vibrator.

She began chuckling, euphoria dancing through her. "Oh, my God, you're so much better than Dean."

Grey rose on his hands, hovering over her, and narrowed his eyes on her. "Saying another man's name while my cock is still buried inside you is not a wise decision, Evie."

She grabbed the vibrator off the bed and held it up. "This is Dean."

The irritation was gone from his expression just that easily, and he chuckled. "You named your vibrator?"

"Yeah, he's Dean Winchester." She laughed at Grey's blank expression. Obviously, he'd never seen the TV show *Supernatural*. "Never mind. All I meant was you're better than the greatest fantasy that I could ever dream up."

He chuckled and withdrew his flaccid cock, grabbing a tissue off her end table and removing the condom, placing it in the trash. After he'd grabbed her sides, pushing her farther up the bed, he slid in next to her. "Well, that's it then."

"What's it?" she asked, boneless.

"To ensure I always keep you happy, I must discover who Dean Winchester is and aim to always be sexier than him."

Evie laughed softly. "Oh, that's quite the feat."

Challenge obviously accepted, Grey leaned in, pressing all that sexy man against her, and his brow arched. "I bet he can't make you do this…" He cupped her sex, and she moaned, melting beneath his hand. His chuckle rushed over her in a heat wave. "See, there's no denying it." With his mouth right by hers, he slid his fingers between her oversensitive folds. She gasped and arched into him, and when she moaned, he took her mouth. His hot, searing kiss quickened her breath, as he added, "The only man you will ever belong to is me."

She arched off the bed, grasping his arm. "Oh, my God, don't stop."

"Tell me, angel," he murmured against her mouth.

She stared into the heat of his eyes, digging her nails into his hot, sweaty flesh. "I'm yours!"

He slid his fingers through her folds, pushing them inside her, and he agreed, "You're damn right you are."

Epilogue

Three years later...

"Dada, a monster."

The hot sun beat down on Grey, sweat trickling over his spine as he held his hands in claws and growled, "Rawr."

Young screams filled the hot, tropical air when Grey chased after the two-year-old fraternal twins, one boy, Mason, one girl, Madison, both *his*. He looked toward where they ran. To their mother.

With green mountains off in the distance, Evie stood near the deep teal-colored ocean, wearing a polka dot tankini with black bottoms. Her arms were open, waiting to save the twins, but they didn't stand a chance. Grey grinned and punched forward, getting to the children first, scooping them up in his arms.

They both screeched, and he pulled them in close, pretending to eat them, and their high-pitched screams made him laugh harder. With a final kiss on both of their heads, he placed them down, and they ran to Evie.

She smiled brightly as they plowed into her, and she hugged them tightly.

In that moment, all Grey noticed was her face. That look of happiness right there was the one he'd sought to see time and time again over the years. Christ, how he loved this woman. How much meaning she'd given to his life.

Hearing a loud laugh behind him, he glanced over his shoulder, finding Maddox sitting in the sand with his four-year-old girl, Sofia, making sand castles. Joss sat next to them, keeping a close eye on their one-year-old boy, Benjamin, who was banging a shovel against the dirt.

Beside them, soaking in the sun in a lounge chair lay his mother, along with her newest husband, a retired multi-millionaire stockbroker out of New York, Warren Ellison. They were sharing cocktails and laughs. And it'd been some time since his mother had genuinely seemed this happy.

The Maui air was good for all of them.

With that thought passing through his mind, Grey's gaze fell on his and Evie's five-bedroom, beachfront house directly on Baby Beach in Lahaina. Stone met dark wood and led to large windows. The house had been built to both blend into the elements and to show off the scenery while inside. With the sandy beach protected by the exposed stretch of reef, the shallow water was perfect for the children. The peacefulness and landscape made this property a given when they'd been looking for the perfect vacation spot.

Grey thought back over the years, realizing how different things were now than they had been when he first met Evie. Even more so, priorities had shifted when children came along. At first, it had been a gradual change, only travelling on weekends and the odd week vacation. Now every winter, they spent as much time as they could in Maui, and less in Seattle.

Both being business owners, Grey and Evie could work remotely, hiring others to handle their jobs in their absence, scheduling meetings every two weeks so they could travel home for a day or two, while Anne cared for the children here in Maui. Life had become more about living, less about working.

Grey had all that he wanted and more.

As laughter once again filled the air, he turned and faced Evie, finding the children running back near the water where their buckets and shovels were waiting for them. While he stayed aware of the kids, he saw Evie approaching, smiling softly at him, the wind waving her damp hair around her face.

He vividly remembered when she'd walked into his office that very first day and changed him as a man. And as she reached him now, he knew without a doubt he wouldn't change one thing about his past. Not their two-month dating relationship before he declared himself a pro and leveled up with a quick proposal. Not him moving into her house. Not even their shotgun wedding three months later.

When Evie stopped in front of him, and he stared into her pretty eyes, she smiled. "You've got that look."

He took one of her hands. "What look?"

"That look like you're thinking about something."

"I am thinking about something," he said, brushing his knuckles across her soft cheek. "I'm thinking about you."

She leaned into his touch and gave him that smile that warmed parts of him that only she had ever touched. He pulled her into his arms, resting his chin on top of her head, and he watched their children scooping up sand into their pails before they ran over to Maddox, helping build the sand castle.

"We're doing a good job with them," Evie said, leaning back to stare up at him. "They're happy, aren't they?"

"Of course, they are." He smiled down at her. "They have the best mother."

Her eyes lightened, the sun making the skin on her face sparkle with the sunscreen. "They've got a very charming father, too, who totally knows how to get lucky."

She stood on her tiptoes, sliding her hands up to his neck, bringing his face to hers. He ran his palms across the small of her back, and she stepped in close as he sealed his mouth over hers. He took charge of the kiss, cupping her face, angling her head to deepen the embrace.

When her tongue slid across his and heat swelled inside him, he chuckled against her mouth. "Better be careful, angel. We have an audience."

She pulled him closer, demanding more of his mouth.

"Momma kissing Dada."

Evie broke away with a laugh. "And there's the bucket of cold water."

Two tiny bodies shoved themselves into the space between Evie and him, and Grey glanced down at them. "Uh-oh, I think I heard something. What's that?" Big, wide, blue eyes greeted him, as he added, "I think the monster's coming back."

"Oh, no," Evie said, grinning down at them, and taking each of their hands. "Run, my darlings, run. Our lives depend on it."

Screams erupted in the air again as the twins ran forward, with Evie in the middle.

Grey roared, "Feed me!" With his toes digging into the sand, he ran forward, and as he did, he looked from his family to the grin on his mother's face to a chuckling Maddox and Joss, and he smiled.

Life was good.

Damn good.

Skirt Chaser
Acknowledgments

Much love to my family; my editor, Christa; my copy editor, Chelle; my assistant, Michelle; the kick-ass authors in my sprint group; and my cover designer, Sara. This book couldn't have happened without all of you!

And thank you to all of YOU, the readers who went on this journey with Maddox and Grey alongside me. I hope Filthy Dirty Love was all that you hoped for and more!

By STACEY KENNEDY

FILTHY DIRTY LOVE
Heartbreaker
Skirt Chaser

DIRTY LITTLE SECRETS
Bound Beneath His Pain
Tied to His Betrayal
Restrained Under His Duty
Cuffed by His Charm (coming soon)

CLUB SIN
Claimed
Bared
Desired
Freed
Tamed
Commanded
Mine

SINGLE TITLES

Five-Alarm Masquerade (anthology, *Hot Shots*)

Rock Star (Bad Boy Homecoming)

Stay up-to-date with Stacey's new releases by visiting these links:

Stacey's newsletter sign-up:
www.staceykennedy.com/newsletter

Website:
www.staceykennedy.com

Facebook:
www.facebook.com/authorstaceykennedy

Stacey's Book Club:
https://www.facebook.com/groups/1031764610185210/

Instagram:
www.instagram.com/staceykennedybooks

Twitter:
twitter.com/Stacey_Kennedy

USA Today bestselling author **Stacey Kennedy** has written more than 30 romances, including titles in her wildly hot Club Sin, Dirty Little Secrets, and Filthy Dirty Love series. Her books are about real people with real-life problems, searching for that special thing we call love... in a very sexy way. When she's not burning up the pages and setting e-readers ablaze, she's living her happily ever after with her husband and two young children in southwestern Ontario. She's a firm believer that wine, chocolate, and sinfully sexy books can cure all of life's problems. To keep in touch with Stacey, get updates right to your inbox at staceykennedy.com/newsletter/.

staceykennedy.com
Facebook.com/authorstaceykennedy
@Stacey_Kennedy

Read on for an excerpt from the first book
in Stacey Kennedy's Club Sin series:

CLAIMED

CHAPTER ONE

"Master Dmitri doesn't expect sex." Cora grunted. "You'll keep your clothes on."

Presley Flynn scanned the foyer of the snazzy mansion and looked for something to hold onto as her roommate, Cora Adams, hustled her down the corridor. With a little shove, Cora added, "You wanted this, remember?"

"Clearly, I've lost my damn mind." Presley pushed back against Cora's hands, trying to hold her ground.

The mansion was pleasant, with thick dark wood on the trim of the doorways and gentle burgundy-painted walls, but it did nothing to settle her nerves. Beneath her feet, located in the basement, was the elite BDSM dungeon, Club Sin. "Maybe I need to go to a therapist. Or skip that part and go straight to the nuthouse."

Cora stepped in front of Presley, and her big blue eyes, lined with dark makeup, sparkled. Her long chocolate-colored hair fell over her black blouse, and her red lipstick covered pursed lips. "You told me you wanted to join the dungeon."

Presley snorted. "You said I was a long-lost submissive who needed the lifestyle. Which, apparently, is so far from the truth, since why am I on the verge of puking all over this fancy hardwood floor?"

Cora smirked. "Please don't puke on Master Dmitri's floor."

"Okay, great," Presley muttered in total agreement. "See, it's best I leave."

She turned to get the hell out of the place when Cora grabbed her arm, pulling Presley back in front of her. "One chance, Presley, that's all you get. If you leave now, you won't be allowed to come back."

Cora walked forward, and Presley found herself matching her stride. They passed a grand wooden staircase on the left, leading to the upstairs. A huge wrought-iron balcony curved around the entire upper floor, which led to numerous doors used for God knew what.

They strode by an oval-shaped dining room, and Cora added, "There's a reason why you read so many BDSM erotic novels. There's a reason why it turns you on. And there's a reason why you made the decision to come with me tonight."

Stopping near the doorway to the office that Presley had been avoiding for the last five minutes, she inhaled. "You're right. I did come here for a reason." To surrender to her every desire. "I don't want to walk out the front door, but—" She pointed toward the office. "I'm scared shitless to walk through that door."

"Of course you are." Cora grinned. "Your darkest, most secret fantasies await you in that office." Without another word, she spun on her heel and headed down the hallway in the opposite direction.

"Do you plan on coming in?"

Presley started at the powerful low voice that seemed to draw her forward, giving the fearful butterflies in her stomach a flutter of excitement. Her feet moved without thought as she entered the office, which looked much like a library.

Books filled the shelves at the far end of the room, along with a grand wooden desk. A computer and telephone and other office accessories sat on top of it. A sleek black leather couch was situated straight ahead, under the bay window.

"Ah, she finally decides to enter."

Presley froze, as time halted. The man never raised his head to look at her, but he didn't need to. His presence filled the room, making her entirely aware of him. He sat at the desk, his head bowed toward the paper he'd been reading. With the slight curve to his mouth, he stole the air from her lungs. He was hot.

As the owner of Club Sin and the president of Las Vegas's top casino, Dmitri Pratt matched the mansion with his wealthy exuberance. Hard angles defined his jawline and cheekbones. His lips were lush and sculpted and his nose straight-edged. The sleeves of his black dress shirt were rolled up on his muscular forearms, displaying a tribal dragon tattoo on his left arm.

When she didn't move, Dmitri stated, with his eyes still focused on the paper, "Take a seat on the couch."

Exhaling slowly, she shed the tension in her chest as she made her way to the leather sofa and sat down. The coolness of the upholstery against her heated skin came as much needed relief. She crossed her legs, doing her best to portray confidence.

In front of this powerful and experienced man, she didn't want to show her apprehension. In fact, she'd never been *this* uncomfortable around men, but Dmitri wasn't simply a man. He sexually dominated women, and as a Dom, he did the kinky things Presley had only dreamed of fulfilling.

He signed the paper, then he lifted his head. Presley forgot the world around her, absorbed in him. His piercing blue eyes gazed over her from head to toe before his focus returned to her face. The depth of those eyes pulled her in with the intensity of how he watched her. No, how he *studied* her. He didn't give her a quick look but a long examination.

Under his stare, her body went mushy and *hot*. Flames flickered through her veins as he stood from his chair and approached. Her fingernails bit into her palms as her heart rate increased. His muscular frame didn't fit his fluid gait. Each step he took exuded authority, like a lion on a hunt, but appeared graceful, with controlled power.

She scanned the thickness of his shoulders beneath his black dress shirt, and she noticed how the fabric clung to him, detailing the valleys of his muscles. Glancing lower, she found the rest of him to be more of the same—powerful and masculine. His black slacks, held tight by a leather belt hung low on his hips, hugged his thick thighs.

Stopping in front of her, he stared at her with impressively intense eyes, and a strand of his stylish blond hair hung across his forehead. "So, you're Cora's friend? Presley, right?"

The commanding nature of his voice made her breathing erratic. This man had the capability of making her feel giddy as a schoolgirl, as if he were her secret crush who'd noticed her at last. "Yes, that's me."

Dmitri's mouth twitched, and he tucked a finger under her jaw, tilting up her chin. "Welcome to my home, Presley."

She shivered at the stern yet gentle hold. "Thank you."

He slid a finger along her jawline, cocking his head, and his study of her touched the center of her soul, awakening her body in a foreign way. As if, for the first time in her life, a man looked at her and truly saw her. His examination made her bare, totally exposed to him, and unusually vulnerable.

Locked in a stare she couldn't break free from, she wiggled in her seat, unable to stop herself, then she froze. After another shift, she couldn't ignore the damp silk between her thighs. How was that even possible—nervous one minute to undeniably turned on the next?

Dmitri's eyebrow arched, and that sexy smile returned. "Pretty little thing, aren't you, doll?"

He removed his hold and she quivered, and her body hummed with desire. The memory of his touch remained. The path his finger had taken was scorched into her skin, and the heat within only intensified as she drew in his masculine scent, edged with sandalwood.

Watching the twinkle in his eyes increase, she cursed herself for being entirely too obvious. Or maybe she should curse him for being so talented at reading people. To calm down, she glanced around the office, looking for something to take her mind off of her response to him.

It was hopeless.

The home seemed like a fairy tale all in itself. Along the dark taupe wall across from her were four huge canvases forming a solid picture of a lone tree and a moon, reminding her that she was out of her element. "That painting is beautiful." *Enormous and expensive.* "Did you pick it out?"

Dmitri followed her gaze for only a moment. "Do I look like the type of man who'd know about art?"

She licked her dry lips, staring at his sculpted mouth that held the mysterious smile, and she admitted, "Kind of."

"No, doll, I couldn't care less about it." He winked. "That's what interior decorators are for."

Dmitri deftly turned and strode toward the watercooler in the corner of the office. Presley frowned at his back. Perhaps she had misread him and he wasn't as fancy as she'd thought, since he seemed amused by her response.

After filling a tall glass with water, he returned to her and offered her the glass. "Here, drink this, love."

"Thanks." She accepted the glass, and settled the cool glass on her lap, not sure she'd get the water down her dry throat.

Dmitri leaned in and gazed into her eyes dead-on. "I didn't give you the glass to hold. I gave you the water because you need it. Drink up, Presley."

The stern set of his jaw indicated he wouldn't relent, so with a shrug, she sipped the water. The cool liquid rushed through her mouth and down her throat, easing the tightness as she swallowed. Maybe she needed that more than she'd thought. He gave a firm nod. "Better."

As he sat next to her on the couch, his thick thigh brushed against hers, and a spark blasted through her, causing her cheeks to warm. The side of his mouth once again curved as he stared at her blush before those intense eyes zeroed in on hers. "Now, then, tell me a bit about yourself."

"Well—" She focused on their conversation and away from how incredible his body felt against hers. "My parents are still together and have a good marriage. I grew up in Apple Valley my entire life, but I moved to Vegas about four months ago to live with my ex." She took another sip of the water and realized she'd almost opened a door she didn't want to go through. Gathering her thoughts, she looked at her hands, clenched around the glass, and continued. "That's a story not worth repeating." No way in hell would she tell him about her ex-boyfriend, Steven Moser, on whom she wasted eight years of her life. "Let's see . . . I'm twenty-five and have no kids."

Dmitri raised his ankle over his knee, drawing her focus to him, and she noticed his body shaking in silent laughter. Maybe, with Steven on her mind, her defenses were already on high alert. Or perhaps Dmitri made her feel way too inexperienced and even too nervous in this erotic adventure she'd entered, but her glare came fierce and instant.

He frowned. "Would you like to try that again?"

"I have nothing else to say." She shifted against the couch, realizing now that she deserved his mirth. In this place, she might as well have a halo over her head. "That's all there is to know about me."

"No, Presley." His eyes were dark, firm, and cold. "In my house, my guests don't glare at me."

Had he honestly noticed her glare? Most times when she glared at Steven, he didn't see it or didn't care enough to ask what had upset her. "I—"

Dmitri's eyes narrowed. "If I've upset you, tell me, so I can address it. Don't give me nasty looks that I don't deserve, considering I've hardly said a word."

The authority in his voice made her insides quiver. It was the meaning in his statement that spoke to something deep inside her—*I see you.* Even if what she'd done bothered him, he didn't overlook any of her actions. For the first time in a long time—possibly ever—she wasn't a shadow, a person everyone passed and never truly looked at, and that made her speechless.

However, at his firm look urging her to continue, she took his advice and asked, "What did you find so funny?"

He dropped his ankle from his knee and turned to face her. "Your little rundown there." His stern expression melted away to a charming smile, drawing her full attention to his kissable mouth. "I didn't mean for you to tell me everything about yourself, as if I were hiring you."

Just kill me now!

His eyes softened, as did his voice. "I meant for you to tell me why you want to join the dungeon, considering you look incredibly nervous."

She almost rolled her eyes but stopped herself. "Right, I guess that's what you'd want to know." Shoving her embarrassment away to fret over later, she put on a brave face and lifted her chin. "Well, I read a lot of erotic romance books and . . . um . . . Cora has told me about the lifestyle, and you see, it . . . "

With a gentle hold, he gripped her chin, tilting her head downward. "Arouses you?"

He dropped his hand and she nodded, and the water in the glass rippled in waves from the tremble of her hands. Gripping it tightly, she bit her lip, which didn't ease the flickers of mortified tremors.

"What about BDSM arouses you?"

His intense study reached into her soul. She squirmed against the leather couch, and her skin flushed wicked hot. "Err . . . the sex stuff."

One sleek eyebrow lifted. "The sex stuff?"

She followed the line of his brow along the masculine contours of his face. While his eyebrow arch looked simple enough, it portrayed a statement of curiosity, and he was beautiful. "You know, being tied up, dominated . . . and um . . . other *stuff*."

Dmitri considered her in a way that made her feel as if he noticed every flaw on her face. "I'm going to be blunt with you, Presley." Before she could inquire what he meant by *blunt*, he added, "I'd appreciate if you stay quiet while I talk. After I'm done, we can discuss what I've told you." He waited for her nod, then he continued. "A Club Sin submissive can be restrained with ropes, cuffs, chains, or anything that can be used to bind a person." His grin became devilish. "Doms enjoy being creative."

Sweet Jesus!

"In a scene, you might be flogged, paddled, whipped, spanked, or caned. You could find yourself tied to a Saint Andrew's cross, tossed over a spanking bench, or attached to any other device located in the dungeon."

Damn her body for flushing at those choices, and damn his wicked expression declaring enjoyment. She took a big gulp of the water, which this time didn't help the dryness in her throat.

His eyes twinkled. "If it's within your limits, you might have intercourse in the dungeon or be asked to give oral sex; if your Dom is especially pleased, you could find yourself climaxing in front of a crowd."

Her mouth dropped open, but he seemed not to realize or care. He added, "This isn't a sex club meant to have vanilla sex. At Club Sin, you are the submissive and are treated as such." Drawing in a deep breath, he allowed her a minute to process before he said, "There are no slaves at Club Sin. We have submissives who, outside of the dungeon, are equal in every regard. In the dungeon, you are the bottom in the relationship and will need to accept that. You don't make decisions. You don't ask questions. You do what your Dom tells you to do."

A shiver slid down her spine. Not at what he said, exactly, but how he said it. The heated look in his eye and the stern tone portrayed a confidence that her lower half appreciated. Which had been part of the battle, excitement at the thought of a man controlling her, yet she'd been raised to have a voice and thoughts. Meshing the two desires and wants was confusing at best.

His head tilted. "Submissives at Club Sin are expected to be submissive only while in a scene. Meaning you're not expected to be in high protocol at all times in the dungeon, as in kneeling at your Dom's feet and avoiding eye contact. These are the rules I've put in place at Club Sin, because they're what I prefer. To be a member, everyone must follow that rule."

He once again let her process it all before he said, "Of course, you are to respect all Doms with proper address; mind your manners; and be respectful to other submissives. But we are not a club that expects high protocol, unless that's something your Dom requires of you for a punishment." That ridiculously sexy eyebrow arched again. "Do you understand?"

Presley nodded and wiggled in her seat, trying to ignore the heat swirling between her thighs. All of what he said were things she'd read about, fantasized over, and the idea that she'd play the submissive role made her burn.

"Some submissives like things others don't, and that's why *you* outline your limits when you sign the dungeon's agreement. That part of play at Club Sin is nonnegotiable. Your limits will never be broken. If you want to change a limit, you'll have a sit-down with me to discuss it. I may agree without hesitation, or I might request that I watch you in scene first if the limit change is drastic." He casually picked a piece of lint off his pants. "What you do in your private life is your business.

Here, in the dungeon, what you do is my business, since I'm the owner of Club Sin. All clear?"

She nodded, managing to close her parted lips, but she was unable to look away from his eyes. There, in their depths, she found something so intoxicating, so centered. Dmitri appeared to be the most put-together man she'd ever met in her life, so sure of himself and his choices, and that was even sexier than his muscular frame and gorgeous face.

He flicked the piece of lint onto the floor. "If you don't follow what has been asked of you, you will be punished. If you refuse your punishment, you will be escorted from the dungeon and not allowed to return."

Her breath became trapped in her throat, and as if he read her concern, he added, "A punishment can be a spanking with a hand or a paddle, a night spent wearing a gag, or whatever the Dom thinks is appropriate for your disobedience. But no punishment would ever exceed your limits. One thing you can count on is your punishment will be fair." He tucked her hair behind her ear, smiling gently. "Now tell me how you feel about what I've told you."

"It's . . . well . . . I . . ." She swallowed, shifting through all the confusion coursing through her veins. Her body burned so hot that she wanted out of her skin. Her mind warned her how insane it was to agree to something that could, in fact, lead to a punishment.

After a moment, she realized the winner of the internal battle was glaringly obvious, because it was why she'd come here tonight. "God forgive me, I liked it."

Dmitri gave her a long look before he threw his head back with laughter. Her embarrassment quickly turned to anger, and she stood so fast that the water spilled on the floor. "Stop laughing at me! This isn't funny."

He slowly looked at her. His eyes had darkened. He rose to his feet with a powerful grace, taking the glass from her hands, and slamming it on the end table with a *clunk*. "To your knees."

In a swift move, she dropped to her knees, cringing when she connected with the hardwood floor. The second the pain eased, she realized what he'd asked and what she'd done.

Had she honestly responded to Dmitri without a single thought? Was she seriously kneeling for the man at his feet? And why had he told her to kneel? Because she snapped at him, or maybe she'd glared again? Her mind raced to understand what had happened in the last couple of seconds, but failed miserably.

Dmitri's shiny black shoes rested in front of her, and his rich masculine scent wrapped around her. He didn't move, nor did he say a word.

She did the only thing she thought would be appropriate in this extremely awkward moment. She whispered, "I'm sorry."

CLAIMED

**A novel of erotic discovery and forbidden desire
that goes beyond *Fifty Shades of Grey*.**

Presley Flynn is ripe to experience her secret fantasies . . . and Dmitri Pratt wants nothing more than to fulfill them. Once inside the elite Club Sin in Las Vegas, Presley is nervous but excited—and determined to surrender to her every desire. Dmitri is her Master, and his touch is like fire. With each careful, calculated caress, he unleashes her wildest inhibitions, giving her unimagined pleasure.

Presley is different than the other submissives Dmitri has mastered. The BDSM lifestyle is new to her, and so are the games they play at Club Sin. From the start, Presley stirs emotions in Dmitri far beyond the raw purity between a dom and the perfect sub. For the ecstasy they share goes beyond the dungeon, igniting a passion that claims the very depths of the heart.

ered*Claimed* is an erotic romance intended for mature audiences.

Find out more in *Claimed*.

Stay up-to-date with Stacey's new releases and join the mailing list:
http://www.staceykennedy.com/newsletter/

Dirty Little Secrets.

Everybody's got 'em . . .

especially the kind of men who have everything.

Check out the first book in Stacey Kennedy's

Dirty Little Secret series . . .

BOUND BENEATH HIS PAIN

The USA Today bestselling author of the Club Sin *novels kicks off a deeply sensual new series by introducing readers to Micah, a man who takes what he wants—until he meets the one woman he needs.*

Real estate mogul Micah Holt exerts absolute control over all aspects of his life. He keeps his dark side hidden away from the press, who will chase down any hint of scandal. He's always in command of his world, careful to expose his closely guarded secrets only to those he knows he can trust. Then Allie Bennett shakes his legendary discipline. She's beautiful, pure, untainted. But is Micah willing to sacrifice her innocence for his own selfish obsessions?

When that sexy smile makes her body burn, Allie tries with all her might to ignore it. For one thing, Micah's her new boss. For another, he's as complicated as he is devastatingly handsome. Still, Allie can only fight so much before she gives in to his dangerous games. She knows he's got dark secrets. But when she discovers the true depth of his pain, Allie must decide how far she's willing to go to light the way for love.

Find out more in *Bound Beneath His Pain.*

Stay up-to-date with Stacey's new releases and join the mailing list:
http://www.staceykennedy.com/newsletter/

9 781635 761474